# BLACK PROMISE

VICTORIA QUINN

## ROME

I was home alone because Calloway went to Ruin. He said he had important business to take care of that he couldn't ignore. He left a guard outside the house to keep an eye on the place so I wouldn't be unprotected.

Even though the guy was a trained professional and had a gun, I still preferred Calloway's protection.

I'd slept with him because I couldn't keep my legs closed any longer. Without any action for six weeks, I had been going crazy. And knowing that big, sexy man was just across the hall from me tested my patience.

So I caved.

Nothing was different between us, and to top it off, Calloway went to Ruin immediately afterward. So the odds of us ever coming to an agreement were slim.

VICTORIA QUINN

I slept in my own bedroom because I had no idea how long he would be gone. The insecure side of me wondered if he was hooking up with a sub at that very moment, some woman who liked to have a chain around her neck. He'd just made love to me, but he might have already jumped into rough sex with someone else.

I had to remind myself Calloway would never do that.

When I woke up the next morning, I was alone in my bed. If Calloway came home, he must have stayed in his own bedroom so he wouldn't disrupt me. I got ready for work like I did every morning then ran into him downstairs.

He looked exhausted, like he was out late last night. In fact, it looked like he hadn't slept at all. "Good morning."

I shouldered my purse. "Morning."

We left together, his driver taking us to the office. As always, we walked inside together, the rest of the employees knowing beyond a doubt we were officially an item. My colleagues didn't talk to me the way they used to, as if they feared anything they said would make its way back to Calloway.

I hated it.

Instead of going to his office like usual, he walked me all the way to mine.

"You don't need to—"

"I want to talk to you after work. It's important." He stood in front of me, brooding with his vibrant blue eyes. In his suit, he looked like a powerhouse. He didn't just own this building, but the entire city.

"Okay…" It must be about the sex we'd had the night before. But I didn't know why he would bring it up now just to leave me hanging all day.

Without another word, he turned around and walked down the hallway, his ass looking tight in his slacks.

The second he was gone, I wanted him to come back. I didn't want to sit in my office all day knowing he was on the other side of the building. I wanted to know what he wanted to talk about—and if it was good news or bad news.

At the end of the day, he arrived at my office. Silent but loud with authority, he leaned against the doorframe as he announced his presence with mere power.

I felt him behind me, so I turned around in my chair to look at him.

He stood with his hands in the pockets of his suit, his shoulders phenomenally broad and powerful. I remembered the way they felt when I dragged my nails down his back. The muscles tensed and coiled underneath my touch.

I grabbed my things and prepared to leave, responding to the silent command he gave me. He was like a caveman, expecting me to read his body language to understand what he wanted. I met him at the door, and we walked out together, my private bodyguard silent with imminent threat.

His driver took us back to his house near the edge of the city. I was tempted to ask him what he wanted to talk about, but since he hadn't mentioned it, I assumed he wanted to wait until we were alone together.

We walked inside, and I slipped off my heels as I usually did, just like when I stayed with him for a few months.

He locked the door behind us and immediately turned on me, his expression dark. It wasn't clear if he was mad or just intense. Lately, I couldn't tell with him. He was so out of his mind with rage that he was unpredictable. "I don't know if I can give you everything you want, like the house with the picket fence and the kids...but I can give you this." He pulled a box out of his pocket and popped it open, revealing a black diamond ring made out of white gold.

I knew he wasn't proposing to me. But I didn't know what he was trying to say either.

"I signed Ruin over to Jackson. It's his now. I have nothing to do with the place."

Now that I knew where this conversation was going, I could hardly breathe. He said he wouldn't give anything up for me. It was impossible for him to do. But here he was, making a compromise I hadn't thought he was capable of making.

"But I want you to wear this, and I'll wear mine. In my world, it's a sign of commitment, fidelity, and loyalty between a Dom and a sub. It means we're monogamous, that we're a pair. You don't have to be my sub. We can be whatever you want us to be. But I want you to wear it regardless. That's my only condition."

I eyed the beautiful ring. The black diamond caught the light and somehow reflected it back. It echoed Calloway's intensity, his constant brooding and adoration. I saw his face the instant I looked at the ring, seeing the band that complemented his so perfectly. "You're giving me what I want?"

"Yes." He pulled the ring out of the box and returned the box to his pocket. "I'll be your boyfriend —nothing else."

I eyed the ring with my hands held to my chest,

realizing this was just as big as a marriage proposal. He was turning his back on his way of life just to keep me, something that was extremely difficult for him. "What changed your mind?"

"Last night." He grabbed my right hand and held the ring to my ring finger. "Is that a yes?"

It was exactly what I wanted. I didn't care that he'd lied to me and had owned Ruin in the first place. I'd missed him so much over these past six weeks that it didn't make a difference to me anymore. I loved this man—forever. "Of course."

He finally slid it onto my finger, moving it past the small knuckle along my finger until it fit snugly against the palm of my hand. He eyed the black diamond sitting on my finger before he brought it to his lips and kissed the back of my hand, his eyes on me the entire time.

I felt a chill run down my spine, a heat sear along every inch of my skin.

He cornered me into the wall then dug one hand into my hair, claiming me with a kiss that stole my breath. His powerful body pressed against me, his chiseled physique feeling like a wall. His fingers latched on to my hair possessively, claiming me as his once more. This time, he wouldn't let me go—not ever.

His other hand unzipped the back of my dress until it came loose. He pushed it off and let the material fall into a pile on the floor. Instead of taking off my panties, he ripped them off with his bare hand. They snapped at the seam, coming apart until they fell on top of my dress.

I pushed his jacket off then loosened his tie. My mouth moved with his, aching to get more of his lips and his tongue. Every time I thought I'd caught my breath, he took it away again. I got his belt undone and finally unfastened his slacks, wanting him to be free.

Once his cock was out, he scooped me up and pinned me against the door. He held me up with his body while one hand remained in my hair. Then he shoved himself inside me, taking my pussy like it was his.

I'd never get used to that enormous cock inside me. It was so big, and I was so small. But I loved every second of the pain, every second of the stretching my body did just to accommodate him.

He fucked me against the wall, his ass tightening with every thrust. I could see our reflection in the mirror on the opposite wall, and I watched his strong body overpower mine. He held me up with ease as if I didn't weigh anything, and he continued to fuck me like we hadn't just made love the night before. "You're mine now. Do you understand me?"

His bossiness came out, but I didn't mind one bit.

VICTORIA QUINN

He'd been mine the entire time we were apart. If he had been with another woman, I would have considered it to be an act of betrayal. "Yes."

"Say it."

I was about to come. I could already feel it. "I'm yours…"

---

We showered together upstairs in his bathroom, the hot water falling down on us and soothing our bodies after the rough sex we had against the wall. I still wore my ring and noticed he never took his off. "Did you start wearing that because of me?"

He rinsed the shampoo from his hair then looked at the black ring on his right hand. "Yes."

"So people would know you were committed to me?"

His eyes found mine, dark and intense. The only answer he gave me was a scorching kiss, the kind with a little bit of lip and a little bit of tongue. He pulled away again and grabbed a bar of soap.

I took the bar from his hand and lathered his chest with it. I loved any excuse to touch him, so I caressed his skin with my fingertips. I moved over his shoulders and down his chest, feeling his underlying strength. His cock was hardening again even though we just had the kind of sex neither one of us would complain about. "So...where do we go from here?"

"I don't know, sweetheart. Wherever we want."

He said he wasn't sure if he could do marriage and kids, but I was sure if I gave him enough time, he would change his mind. We had to take it day-by-day, one step at a time. "You'll be able to handle vanilla all the time?"

He watched me rub the soap against his body, the suds dissolving into his skin. "I'll do my best. It's better than living without you. After six weeks of that, I couldn't handle it anymore. I would much rather try to make this work than find someone else that means nothing to me."

My hands faltered as I rubbed the soap into his skin, touched by what he said. "You didn't have to give up Ruin for me. I've never really had a problem with it, just with your demand to make me your sub." My hand moved again, trailing the soap down his hard chest and even harder stomach.

"It's not a good environment for me. It'll only tempt me." He grabbed the soap from my hand then rubbed me down instead, lathering it into my skin and massaging my tits like they were filthy. "I'm sure

Jackson will do fine. And if he doesn't, he can always call me."

It was still hard to believe that he'd done this for me. "Are you sure about this?"

Calloway's hand moved to my chin, and he lifted my gaze until I was forced to look at him. "All I know is I can't lose you. So if this is what I have to do, I'll do it."

---

I was now the black sheep at Humanitarians United. I was no longer invited to lunch with the rest of the staff, and anytime I walked into a room, the conversation died down like they'd just been talking about me.

It sucked.

I suspected things would be difficult once they knew I was sleeping with Calloway, but I didn't expect everything to change so dramatically. They'd all liked me before they knew about my personal relationship with the boss. I was still a great worker who was passionate about my job. I gave a hundred percent at all times. But that didn't seem to matter to them.

Now I was just the boss's squeeze.

At lunchtime, Calloway visited my office. He leaned against the doorframe and announced himself quietly.

I picked up on his presence because there was abundant electricity in the air. It seared my skin and made me hot everywhere. I turned around and faced him, seeing him look like a model in his black suit. "What can I do for you, Mr. Owens?"

His gaze turned a shade darker, a shade more threatening.

I knew I'd said the wrong thing.

"We're going to lunch." He nodded in the direction of the hallway. "Now."

I really hated being told what to do, but since everyone was around, I didn't argue with him. They already hated me, and I didn't want to give them any reason to hate me more. I grabbed my purse and walked into the hallway with him. Once we were in the elevator, I spoke my mind. "I don't like being told what to do."

He kept his hands in his pockets and stood on the other side of the elevator, purposely keeping his distance from me. "That's too bad."

"Too bad?" I asked coldly. "What's that supposed to mean?"

The elevator continued to descend to the bottom floor. "I've given up my lifestyle for you, in case you've forgotten. You can let me be dominant in other ways.

When I say we're going somewhere, we're going somewhere."

"I didn't agree to that," I snapped. "You said you would be my boyfriend."

"I am your boyfriend." He turned to me, his gaze cold. "I'll do everything you ask. But don't expect me to change who I am. Besides, I know you like it."

"Then why am I so pissed right now?"

He shrugged. "As if I have a clue."

I rolled my eyes. "Just don't do it at work." I had to admit, I did like it. I liked it when he told me to bend over so he could fuck me. I liked it when he told me to cuddle into his side while we slept. Sometimes, it got my engine going. But other times, like now, I didn't care for it. "Okay?"

He looked forward again, waiting for the doors to open now that we were on the bottom floor.

"Okay?" I pressed.

He wore an arrogant smile, a slight one that was hardly noticeable. He walked out first then held the door open for me. His silence suggested the conversation was finished—to him.

I kept my outrage to myself and walked out.

We left the building then reached the sidewalk. Calloway kept walking like he knew exactly where he was going. We crossed the street then entered the lobby of a beautiful hotel.

"Do they have a restaurant here?"

Calloway approached the front desk without answering my question. "Reservation for Owens."

Reservation?

The clerk did a few things on the computer before he handed over a room key. "Enjoy your stay, sir."

"Thank you." Calloway took my hand and pulled me into the elevator.

"What are we doing?"

The elevator rose several floors before the door opened again. "We're gonna fuck, and then we're gonna have lunch." He grabbed my hand and pulled me into the hallway. He located the room and got the door open. Inside was a fancy suite, something too nice to only be used during a lunch hour.

"You're being serious." Calloway wasn't the joking type, but this was extreme for him.

"Absolutely, sweetheart." He picked up the phone and ordered two random entrees from the menu. "Have it here in twenty minutes." He hung up then turned back to me, already undoing his tie around his corded neck. His muscular hands worked quickly, dropping pieces of clothing on the floor.

"We've never done this before."

"No, we haven't. But things are different now." He walked up to me and guided me backward until my knees hit the foot of the bed.

"Different how?"

"You know what kind of man I am. You know what kind of needs I have. I haven't had you in six weeks, and now I need to catch up." He yanked up my skirt then pushed me back onto the bed. "Or would you rather I fuck you on my desk at the office? Honestly, that's what I prefer. But I figured you'd rather have it this way." He pulled my panties off but left my heels on. The bed was elevated, so it was the perfect level for his hips. He dragged me to the edge and dropped his slacks and boxers to the ground.

Now that his gorgeous cock was right against my entrance, I didn't care about how unprofessional we were both being. I wanted his length inside me, to feel the stretch that always made me a little sore afterward. "I just want you inside me. I don't care where."

His eyes darkened, and the corner of his mouth rose in an arrogant smile. "That's my sweetheart." He pressed his head inside me and greeted my wetness with his own. Slowly, he slid inside me, stretching me wide apart as his cock marked its territory. His hands gripped the backs of my knees as he spread my legs. A loud moan issued from his throat as he sank every inch into me. "Your pussy is always so tight."

My hands gripped his hips, and I pulled him into me as he thrust, working together to feel each other as much as possible. It started off slow and gentle, both of us appreciating the sensations between us. But then it erupted into ruthless fucking, both of us eager to get more of each other.

I loved the way he pinned me at the edge of the bed, keeping me stationary while he worked his body to fuck me. He was so desperate to have me that he took me across the street during our lunch hour just to fuck. That made me feel desirable and unbelievably sexy. Calloway didn't just say pretty lines to make me feel beautiful. He always touched me and showed me how attracted to me he truly was.

His eyes locked to mine, looking like a king as he stood tall over me. His impressive length continued to fit inside me, forcing my body to accommodate him. "I love looking at you." He tightened my knees against my waist, keeping me wide open for his cock to enjoy.

My hands wrapped around his wrists so I had something to grab on to. His pulse thudded against my fingertips, powerful and strong. I could feel his arousal through the strong beat, the vibration against my fingertips. Everything about that moment turned me on, aroused me to exceptional new heights. "Calloway…"

He released his left hand and grabbed my right one, interlocking our fingers together so he could feel the ring he'd given me. Once he touched the metal, his gaze darkened and took on a new intensity.

My orgasm was unexpected. It came in a rush, striking my body all over and making me writhe. I arched my back as the sensation rocked through me, and the scream that accompanied it must have reached our neighbors next door. I gushed around his cock, my come sheathing his length.

He leaned over me, his strong arms holding his massive body on top of mine. He ground his hips harder into me, his body rubbing against my throbbing clitoris. He gave me a final kiss, slow and seductive, just before he released inside me. He inserted his entire length into me, nearly hitting my cervix, and he dumped all of his arousal inside me. His eyes were glued to mine, wanting to watch me fill up with his come. A quiet moan burst from the back of his throat as he finished. "Fuck…"

I gripped his hips as I kept him within me, wanting to feel our connection for a moment longer. Soon, room service would arrive, and we'd have to return to work. But for now, I could enjoy his cock just a little longer.

He didn't touch my hair like he usually did,

probably not wanting to mess it up before I returned to the office. He kissed me again, his cock softening inside me. "I want you to feel my come for the rest of the day."

"I do too…"

His eyes narrowed on my face, clearly pleased by that response. He leaned down and kissed me on the forehead, his kiss warm and his smell intoxicating, then he pulled his cock out as he stood.

The second he was gone, I felt like I was missing a piece of myself.

A knock sounded on the door. "Room service."

Calloway took his time putting on his clothes, not rushing for anyone.

I walked into the bathroom and shut the door, too much of a mess to be seen by anyone. I heard Calloway open the door and take the tray before the delivery man left. "He's gone, sweetheart."

I came out, my hair fixed and my dress smoothed out. I could feel the weight of his come still sitting inside me, heavy and warm.

Calloway had the table set up in front of the large window that overlooked the city. There were two glasses of water along with our entrees. He'd ordered salads and sandwiches for both of us. He came to my side of the table and pulled out my chair just like he would at a restaurant. He'd just screwed me at a hotel in the middle of his lunch hour, but he treated me like a queen a moment later.

He sat across from me and sipped his water, his jaw chiseled and defined. His gaze was less brooding, less intense now that he got what he wanted out of me. He started with his salad first and ate quietly, his gaze moving to mine once in a while.

I ate in silence, having nothing to say now that we'd already had a full conversation with our bodies.

"How is everyone treating you?"

I cracked a sarcastic laugh. "They all hate me, Calloway. And you know that."

He took a bite of his sandwich and took his time chewing. He didn't inhale his food like most men I knew. There was no way in hell he would be built like a Roman soldier if he ate too much. "That's a shame. I'm sorry to hear that."

I shook my head because I didn't know what to say. "I knew it would happen once we paraded it around the office like that."

"We didn't parade anything. It's not like I fucked you in the middle of the conference room during a meeting."

"We made it just as obvious. We always come in together. We leave together. And if anyone watched us go to lunch, they would have seen us check in here."

"So what?" he asked coldly. "We keep it professional at the office. They shouldn't treat you differently just because you're sleeping with me. It doesn't affect your working ability."

"But it affects my work ethic."

He took another bite, taking his time. "If anyone takes it too far, let me know. I'll fire them."

Even if they treated me like shit, I would never tell Calloway. I wouldn't take advantage of my relationship with him just to make my life easier. That wasn't why I was with him, and I never wanted him to question my feelings.

"It'll die down after a while. They'll get used to it."

"Hopefully." I suspected they'd always be hesitant around me. I was loyal to Calloway, so they were afraid to tell me anything, worried I would leak the information to him. Now I was the office snitch—the office slut.

"Don't let it bother you." He moved his hand to mine on the table, and his large hand gave mine a gentle squeeze. They were covered in masculine veins, their power obvious by the sight of the muscle underneath.

I felt warm once he touched me that way, embraced me like I was the only woman he cared about. My mouth rose in a smile, and I flicked my thumb over his hand. "Thanks…"

He brought my hand to his lips and placed a gentle kiss over my knuckles, his warm breath falling on my skin. His eyes remained locked to mine, full of affection as well as attraction. "Besides, you can always be my private secretary if things don't work out." He waggled his eyebrows before he dropped my hand.

"I'm pretty sure I already am your private secretary —at home."

## 2

## CALLOWAY

I wasn't happy about giving up the only life I'd ever known. But I couldn't live without Rome anymore. Something about this woman changed me. She strengthened me when I was already powerful. She pushed me when I couldn't be pushed any further. She made me feel more like a man because she was an incredible woman.

I had to give it a try.

We came home after work, entering the empty house we both shared. She was staying with me temporarily—at least, that's what she thought. I had very different plans for our arrangement.

She slipped off her heels by the door—as always.

I'd come to love her little habits, the things she did without even realizing it. I loved the way she brushed her teeth at night before bed. I loved the way she ran her fingers through her wet hair just before she dried it. I loved the fact that she looked just as beautiful without makeup as she did when she got dressed up.

And I loved the way she looked wearing that ring. The black diamond looked perfect against her pale skin. I loved officially claiming her, making her mine forever. Now that I'd seen her wear that ring of commitment, there was no way I could let her go.

The second we were alone together behind locked doors, I wanted to do the thing I loved most. I wanted her on her back, her thighs spread and her ankles locked together around my waist. I pressed her into the wall and kissed her, the exact place where I fucked her the other day. My hands moved to the wall and boxed her in, making sure my prey couldn't escape.

She clearly didn't want to run. She melted at my touch right on cue, her hands moving to my powerful arms. The quiet sounds she made when she kissed me were sexy. I didn't need to stick my fingers in her pussy to know she was wet for me.

I knew I should head to the gym after work and get back to a routine, but I didn't want to leave Rome alone. In fact, I didn't want to leave her at all. I wanted to fuck her all day and all night. My woman was back in my life, and I didn't want to waste a moment doing something else when I could be buried inside her.

I picked her up and carried her upstairs to my bedroom on the third floor. I placed her on the bed gently then began to peel her clothes away. That afternoon, I just lifted up her dress and rammed my cock inside her. But now I wanted to take my time, get her naked so I could truly enjoy her.

When she was naked on the bed, I considered her perfect figure. She had nice tits, a tiny waist, and flawless skin. The demon inside me wanted to smack my palm against the delicate flesh and mark it red. The arousal flooded through me at the thought, and I was gripped by the memory of a leather belt in my hand. But I pushed it away and concentrated on the sensual sex I was about to have.

I undressed myself, taking my time to torture her. I slowly worked my tie and loosened it around my neck.

She squirmed on the bed, licking her lips with arousal burning in her eyes.

I dropped my tie on her stomach then undid each button of my shirt, slowly revealing my chiseled physique.

"Come on…"

Nothing sexier than watching a woman beg. "Touch yourself while you wait."

She moved her hand between her legs and rubbed her clit in a circular motion. At the first touch, her

VICTORIA QUINN

breathing hitched. She arched her back as her thighs fell away, her breathing increasing noticeably.

I got to the last button, my cock hard as steel in my slacks. I watched her hand rub that little nub and excite herself even more. She was touching herself to me, getting off to me stripping. I moved to my pants next, forcing myself to go slow even though I wanted to get naked as quickly as possible.

She parted her lips when she moaned, her hand working harder against her clit. Her chest blushed a beautiful pink color, and her nipples hardened to the edge of knives.

I undid my slacks quickly and pushed them down along with my boxers, unable to maintain my slow pace. I kicked off my shoes and didn't bother with the socks. "You're so goddamn sexy, sweetheart." I crawled on top of her and placed her feet against my chest, pinning her underneath me so there was nowhere for her to go.

She gripped my hips and pulled me into her, just as anxious for me as I was for her.

I loved the way she looked in that moment, so desperate to have me. Her obsession matched my own. This woman was my driving force for everything. She was my whole world, my whole universe. And I knew she felt the same way about me.

I sank into her, slowly giving her every inch until she had all of me.

"Oh god…" Her hands snaked to my biceps, her favorite muscle to grab on to.

She was always so tight. It didn't matter how many times I fucked her or how rough I gave it to her. Her pussy was just too small, and my cock was just too big. I rocked into her slowly to get her used to me. Every time we screwed, I needed to ease her into it, to give her body time to stretch to accommodate my large size. Otherwise, I would just hurt her.

And that was the last thing I wanted to do.

---

I was at work when my PI called me.

"What's up, John?" I said into the speakerphone. My eyes were glued to the window, seeing the rest of the city as my backdrop. This city was full of people trying to make their dreams come true, trying to make something of themselves.

"Hank is pretty transparent. Went to Dartmouth for undergrad then Columbia for his law degree. He's been a public figure for a long time. His father used to be the mayor of New York City. His mom was a fashion model. He's done a lot for the community as the DA.

Put a lot of bad guys behind bars, criminals that killed cops. He's pretty much a hero in the eyes of the city."

That wasn't what I wanted to hear.

"Other than that, he's squeaky-clean. Nothing on his record."

Even worse.

"Sorry, Mr. Owens. I know that wasn't what you wanted to hear."

When I thought about the heinous shit he did to Rome, I knew she couldn't be the only one. He had to have stalked and assaulted other women. It tended to be a pattern for men like him. "Look into all of his old girlfriends. I want their names and addresses. Everything."

"Of course, sir." He hung up.

I let the line go dead before I hit the button on my phone and ended the call. I continued to stare out my window and tried to control the rage that swept through me like a forest fire. I wasn't just angry—I was insane. My hands tightened into fists, and my knuckles turned white. When I thought about what that asshole did to my woman, it made me see red. Rome was my whole world. If anyone touched her, they were asking for their own execution.

Even though I was happy to be reunited with her, that joy was fleeting. Once I was alone, my thoughts immediately turned to the man I'd proclaimed as my enemy. I'd seen his face, and it haunted my dreams. Sometimes my nightmares showed him on top of Rome, thrusting inside her with a maniacal gleam in his eyes. I started thrashing in bed until Rome woke me up. Every time she asked what my nightmares were about, I never answered.

If anything ever happened to her...I wouldn't be able to go on.

I wouldn't be able to forgive myself for not protecting her.

Hank reminded me of my own father. He was psychotic, violent, and evil. I didn't stand up to my father until way later than I should have. But I wasn't making that mistake again. Hank had been obsessed with Rome for far too long.

I needed to put him down.

My secretary's voice came through the phone. "Mr. Owens, Christopher is on the line to speak with you."

I hit the intercom button. "Thanks. I'll take it." I hit the speakerphone button and addressed him. "What a nice surprise." Christopher and I had been on decent terms since the shit hit the fan. He didn't like me as much as he used to, but he tolerated me.

"Since you're with Rome 24/7, I knew I'd have to call on my lunch break if I wanted some privacy."

I definitely didn't let Rome out of my sight — not even for a second. "Hank hasn't tried anything. He probably doesn't know where to look for her. Has he come by the apartment?"

"Not from what I can tell. But I'm sure he has men watching the place. He's probably figured out that she's not staying here anymore."

If he had men watching her, that was truly creepy. "You're always welcome to stay at my home if you aren't comfortable, Christopher." He wasn't the kind of man to admit he was afraid, but I wanted to make the offer anyway.

"I'm fine," he said with confidence. "He doesn't want me, so I doubt I'll hear from him again."

"Unless he wants to figure out where she is." I knew this wasn't over. I was prepared for anything at this point. If Hank had gone all the way to her apartment and broken in during the middle of the day, he obviously thought he was invincible.

"I'll never talk. Maybe we can get away with assault and harassment, but even the DA can't get away with murder. I'm not afraid of him."

Neither was I. "If you ever change your mind, let me know."

"Are you kidding me? I have a huge bachelor pad all to myself now. The ladies love it."

I chuckled into the phone. "Sounds like things worked out for you."

"Some good came out of it. I didn't want to live with Rome in the first place. Now she's your problem."

She was the best problem I'd ever had.

"So...does that mean you guys are back together?" There was no hope or dread in his voice. His feelings about the matter weren't clear like they usually were.

"Yeah."

"Oh...I'm surprised Rome changed her mind."

"I caved." I didn't feel ashamed about it anymore. Having her sleep with me every night made it all worth it. I loved the sex, no matter how vanilla it was. I loved everything about her even though I had no control over her. I would rather have this than my previous misery.

"Meaning?"

"I gave up Ruin. I gave up the lifestyle."

"Wow...I didn't think you could do it. You stood your ground for six weeks."

"That was the best I could do. After what happened to her...I understood how much she meant to me." Knowing Hank laid a hand on her sent me into a terrifying rage. That wouldn't have happened if she had been sleeping with me. No one would ever bother her again if she were mine. I couldn't let that ever happen again. Forsaking my old ways was a small price to pay to keep her safe. I really didn't have much of a choice. If I didn't give her what she wanted, she would move out eventually and be left vulnerable to another attack.

"Yeah, I get it. I've never felt that way about a woman, but I can imagine. I was pretty upset when everything went down. Rome is a good person. She doesn't deserve to be stalked and nearly raped just because she's beautiful. It's disgusting."

I couldn't think about the implications of Hank's success. If Rome hadn't been a hard-ass and fought him off, he would have gotten his way—taking something that didn't belong to him. Then I really would have killed him. Rome's strength was the reason I wasn't sitting in jail at that very moment. "Yeah..."

"Thanks for being there for her. I do my best to look out for her, but I'm not you. I don't have the same kind of power."

"I don't mind." Rome meant everything to me. Since the moment she walked into my life, everything had been better. She made me happy when I didn't think I could be. I'd give her the entire world if I could. "She'll be safe with me. Between you and me, I hope Hank comes after me. I would love to kill him."

"Yeah, that makes two of us."

We ate dinner together in comfortable silence. It was the third night we were eating leftovers since Rome refused to throw anything out. She would eat anything unless it was so spoiled it would actually make her sick.

Since she was so passionate about it, I didn't mind.

We made small talk about work and discussed the next charity benefit we were having at the Four Seasons, but I didn't really listen to her. I was more absorbed in her features, watching the way her lips moved when she spoke. Her green eyes weren't quite as bright as they used to be. There was a distinct melancholy about her, a sadness she struggled to hide.

"Something on your mind?" I ignored my glass of wine because I wished it were scotch instead. I put away the hard liquor once she moved back in with me because she made her feelings about it pretty clear. I wasn't allowed to be a drunk when she was around—in my own home. But the more authority she showed, the more obsessed I became. I was drawn to her power like a moth to a flame.

"No." She kept her eyes down, a guilty sign.

"Don't lie to me." I didn't mean to come off so harsh. It was difficult for me to be gentle when I was concerned. I wanted her to be completely open with me —no more secrets. She should have told me everything about Hank before things got this bad.

She looked up again, the hardness in her eyes. She always fought me out of principle, but she loved my authority at the same time. Sometimes, I wondered if she even realized it. "Have you thought about what we're going to do about Hank?"

Other than kill him, not really. "My PI got some information on him. His record is squeaky-clean. But he's got skeletons in his closet like any other politician. And I'll find them."

"What do you know about him?"

"He went to the best schools. His father was the mayor for a long time. He's put away a lot of cop-killers. He's pretty much the face of this city."

"I was afraid of that…" She took a bite then sipped her wine.

"But this behavior couldn't have started with you." Rage burned up inside me again, and I had the urge to knock the table over. My hands formed fists on the table, and I forced them to relax. "He must have a history of assault and abuse. I'm looking into his old lovers to see if I can find anything."

"And do what?"

"Get them to come forward," I explained. "Maybe the word of one woman isn't enough, but when there are several, it really makes a difference."

"That's true…"

"So we'll go the legal route. But if that doesn't work..."

She watched me, her gaze full of hesitance. "Then what?"

I didn't finish the sentence because I didn't need to.

"We aren't going that route. That's not a solution."

My temper flared, and I couldn't control it. "I'm running the show, Rome. We'll do whatever I see fit. This is my problem, and trust me, I will fix it."

She didn't like that answer one bit. "Killing him isn't the answer. You could lose everything, Calloway."

"But you would be free." She wouldn't have to look over her shoulder every time she walked down the street. She wouldn't have to make sure the door was locked ten times before she could sleep at night. She would never have to worry about that man coming after her again. That would make it all worth it.

Her eyes softened like I'd said something funny. "I don't want that, Calloway. I don't want you or Christopher to get in trouble because of my mistake."

"It wasn't a mistake, Rome. How were you supposed to know he was a psychopath? He purposely misled you. Don't apologize for that."

She looked down at her plate again.

"In my experience, these problems don't go away unless someone dies."

"Calloway, stop talking like that."

"It's the truth." I clenched my jaw in irritation. "This is just a sick game to him. He's obsessed, and he's not going to stop until he wins. That's how it goes. He's the predator, and you're the prey. But I'm a bigger predator, so now he's the prey." I grabbed the wineglass and drank all of it, needing all the alcohol in my system even if it was weak. I could really go for some scotch right now, but that would get Rome all fired up.

Rome set down her fork and pushed her plate away, obviously finished with her dinner. But there were still a few bites left.

Now I knew something was seriously wrong. "Sweetheart, talk to me." Did I say something to upset her? Did I take it too far? Maybe I shouldn't have worn my rage so well, made it so visible.

"I just…" She ran her hand through her hair, pulling the soft brown strands away as she kept her eyes averted.

I waited in dread, unsure what she was going to say.

"I guess that whole thing is really hitting me. I've never taken the time to sit down and think. I've never had the opportunity to feel safe, so I just kept pushing forward. I never had any choice in the matter, so I just dealt with it."

I didn't really understand what she was saying, so I

remained quiet, hoping she would become clearer on her own.

"But now that I have you…I feel safe." She kept her head bowed like she couldn't look at me. "And now that I know what that feels like, I don't want to be scared anymore. I'm more scared of being scared… I know I'm not making any sense right now. But when he dragged me into the apartment, I was so afraid I was going to lose. I was afraid he would overpower me and…I knew how much that would hurt you."

I kept a straight face to make this easier on her, not wanting her to see my pain.

"I just want it to stop, you know?" she whispered. "Only when I'm in this house do I really feel like no one will hurt me. Only when you're sleeping next to me do I feel protected. I love feeling that way, but I hate relying on someone to make me feel that way. I feel like I don't have any freedom, any power." She ran her fingers through her hair again, her eyes wet.

I stood up and moved to the chair directly beside her. My arm hooked around her, and I pressed my face close to hers, comforting her in the best way I could. "It will stop, sweetheart. I promise."

"I know…"

"And he's never going to succeed, Rome. He's never going to bother you again. As long as I'm breathing, he'll never lay a hand on you. You can enjoy feeling safe because I'll continue to make you safe." I brushed her hair off her forehead then kissed her temple.

"I know you will, Calloway. I just… I've always taken care of myself. I hate having to rely on someone else. It's not in my nature. I feel like an embarrassment to women everywhere."

"Don't say that."

"But I do. I don't want to run to the shelter of a man. I want to fight my own battles."

"Everyone needs help, sweetheart. It has nothing to do with the fact that you're a woman. We all need to band together to reach our goals sometimes. You aren't relying on me to do anything. I'm looking after you because—" The words died in my throat before I could say them, before I could do something incredibly stupid. "I'm looking after you because I can't live without you, Rome. We're a team. We're in this together." I kissed her temple again, my lips warm against her cold skin. "We will find a solution. I promise you." My hand cupped her neck, and I rested my thumb against her gently beating pulse. I pressed my mouth against hers and gave her a slow kiss, full of affection and devotion. I wanted her to feel safe with me because there was nowhere else in the world that she would be safer. I didn't need guns or knives to protect her. All I needed was my body and my bare hands.

---

I was dead asleep when Rome rolled hard into my side, her hand lashing out and striking me right in the back of the head.

I sat upright and looked down at her, my eyes lidded and heavy with sleep. I dragged my hand down my face so I could get a better look at her, my eyes taking a moment to adjust to reality.

Tears streaked down her face as she continued to whimper under her breath, saying wordless phrases in the throes of a nightmare.

"Sweetheart." I grabbed her shoulder and shook her gently. "Come on, you're having a nightmare." I shook her again when my words weren't enough to wake her up. "Rome." I said it more firmly, using her name to pull her out of the terror she was experiencing.

She finally sat up and gripped her chest as she gasped, taking in a deep breath like it was the first time she could access air. When she felt the tears, she quickly wiped them away as if she was embarrassed. She stared into the dark room like she was trying to figure out where she was.

"Rome, it's okay." My arm hooked around her, and I pressed into her side. "It was just a nightmare. That's all."

She pulled her knees to her chest and concentrated on slowing her breathing, forcing herself to calm down.

I pressed a kiss to her shoulder and allowed my affection to heal her, to remind her she was safe with me. "It's just you and me. No one else." I rubbed her back and continued to kiss her, to let my adoration seep through her skin and directly into her core. "Alright?"

All she did was nod.

I kissed the back of her neck then her hairline, giving her more affection to lull her back into relaxation. I lay back down and then patted the mattress beside me.

She eyed the spot before she crawled across my chest, getting so close to me there wasn't any space between us. My body heat encompassed her, bringing her back into the security my strong frame provided. "I'm sorry…"

"Shh, it's okay." I ran my hand through her hair as I held her close to me.

"I don't usually have nightmares."

"It happens to the best of us."

"Did I hurt you?"

"No." I pressed my mouth against hers, giving her a

seductive kiss that changed the course of her thoughts. Feeling her cling to me for comfort only aroused me. I loved hearing that she needed me, that I made her feel safe when no one else in the world could. I loved seeing her trust me, knowing I would risk my own life to protect hers. In that sense, it reminded me of the Dom/sub relationship that I missed, where my partner trusted me completely to give her what she needed.

Now I was hard, but there was nothing I could do about it.

I kept kissing her until I felt the strength to pull away. Rome just had a nightmare, and it would be insensitive for me to automatically take it to sex, not when she was obviously still upset.

Rome stared at my lips once they were gone, her lidded eyes looking beautiful in the dark. She moved back into me and kissed me again, her lips aching for mine. Her smell washed over me, her hand gripping me like she needed me. Then she pulled me on top of her, her leg hooking around my waist.

Once I felt my cock rub against her wet pussy, all my sensitivity went out the window. My woman wanted me—and there was no way in hell I was going to say no.

# 3

## ROME

I wasn't prepared for the nightmare that came to me the night before. Hank was the star, and he gripped me by the neck and bent me over the bed, raising my dress and removing my panties with force.

I didn't see the end because Calloway woke me up.

Thank god.

I got ready the following morning and had a little pep talk with myself. Last night, I was weak and let that vulnerability show when I shouldn't have. I admitted I was scared, and that confession made Hank the victor. I'd been taking care of myself for a long time, and so far, I'd managed to keep my head above water.

I would continue to do so.

Even without Calloway by my side, I wouldn't let Hank get to me. I wouldn't allow him to take something that didn't belong to him. If I had to, I would kill him and suffer the consequences later.

Calloway and I rode in the back of his car on the way to work. He moved his hand to my thigh and rested it there, his palm heavy from pure masculinity. He kept his gaze outside of the car and didn't question me about the night before. He never asked what my nightmare was about—probably because he figured it out on his own.

We arrived at the building, and Calloway opened the door for me like he did every morning. He didn't take my hand or put his arm around my waist now that we were outside the office.

Together, we walked to the entryway, practically a mile apart. Calloway wore a dark suit, looking magnificent like always. His face was cleanly shaven, and his exposed chin made me want to trail kisses all down his jawline.

But I kept my hands to myself.

As we approached the door, I felt a malicious gaze fall on my body. The look was scorching, evil. Deep down inside, I knew who it was before I even looked. I turned my head and locked eyes with the man who was committed to ruining me.

That fucking asshole.

Calloway kept moving to the door, but my rage took

over and I did something stupid. I marched over to Hank with my hand balled into a fist. If he thought he could do something on my way to work, he was an idiot. I'd kick his ass right in front of the building for the whole world to see. "You fucking asshole."

Hank smiled like this was a game. "I was just in the neighborhood and wanted to stop by. Nice to see that you cleaned up well."

I launched my fist at his face immediately.

Hank caught it and lowered it back to my side, using his strength to overpower me. His eyes were absorbed in my expression, so he didn't notice Calloway behind me, who was probably about to murder Hank right this second.

A shadow passed over me, and that's when I knew Calloway was officially in the mix. He moved right past me, forcing me to the side when his massive frame squeezed me out of the picture. He was taller than Hank, so he had to look down at him slightly, his eyes brooding and threatening. He didn't say a single word to Hank, just warned him with a simple look.

Hank didn't back down, but he didn't make the mistake of throwing a punch. He eyed Calloway, sizing up his opponent before he determined what to do next. He was in his suit, probably on his way to work at the DA's office.

Calloway took a step forward.

Hank automatically took a step back, his arms tense by his sides. Calloway was a much bigger adversary than I was. His punches couldn't be easily stopped with a simple block. When Hank's face paled to a milky white color, it was obvious he didn't like the turn of events.

Calloway knew better than to attack Hank right out in the open like this. There were witnesses everywhere, and it would be easy to control the narrative and say Calloway started an unprovoked fight. Since Hank was an experienced lawyer, it was a path Calloway couldn't take.

Hank stepped back again, obviously uncomfortable by the maniacal gleam in Calloway's eyes. I'd been the victim of that stare before, and I knew how terrifying it was. Calloway didn't have to say a single word to express his feelings. They were quite clear. Yet he let one slip. "Run."

Hank faltered backward as he tripped over his own feet. His hand caught his body on the concrete, and he quickly got up again, dirtying the back of his suit. He didn't run like Calloway recommended, but he definitely didn't take his time getting to the road and waving down a cab.

Calloway watched him the entire time, his shoulders

tense and his arms tight. His eyes followed the car until it was completely out of sight. Even then, he kept searching for Hank like he might return. His jaw was clenched tight, and his eyes were full of imminent threat.

I'd never seen Hank take off like that. Every time I threatened him, it just spurred him on. He clearly didn't see me as a threat, but when it came to Calloway, it was a completely different story.

We entered the building and took the elevator to our floor. Calloway stayed on one side of the elevator, his hands in his pockets and his gaze concentrated on the wall in front of him. He didn't make any effort to comfort me. He was focusing on keeping himself calm before the doors opened and his employees looked at him.

We stepped out and walked by everyone's desks like usual. One hand was in his pocket, and he held his head high as he walked. When we were past everyone, he spoke.

"My office," Calloway said darkly. "Now."

I didn't object.

We walked inside, and he locked the doors behind us, not caring if people thought we were screwing. He walked to his desk and stood in front of it, his shoulders broad and rigid. He gave a violent shout before he tossed all the contents off the desk, breaking his computer and everything else.

I crossed my arms over my chest and stood silent, knowing any sound would just make it worse.

Calloway paced the office space before he leaned against the desk, gripping the edge until his knuckles turned white. He stared at me with blue eyes that burned hotter than white-hot flames. His chest rose and fell with deep breaths, his recklessness unable to be tamed.

I slowly approached him like he was a wild animal that could be spooked at any time. I placed my hands against his chest and ran them down slowly, touching him the way I did when we were in the shower together.

Calloway calmed slightly when he felt my touch. His breathing slowed once he felt the pressure of my fingertips. He stared down at my hands and closed his eyes for a moment before he opened them again.

"I've never seen Hank do that before..." I was in awe that Calloway had scared him off so easily. He didn't even need to say anything. All he had to was flex his muscles and give an ice-cold look. He'd done something I didn't think anyone could accomplish. "He's scared of you."

"He recognized me."

My hands moved to his arms, gripping his biceps. "How do you know?"

"I could just tell," he said quietly. "He recognized the building, and put two and two together. I may not be the DA, but I'm pretty well-known in this city. He knows I'm not someone he should cross."

I massaged his arms and felt the relief wash through me, the first time I ever thought Hank might actually disappear. All these years I'd been running from Hank, when all I needed was Calloway to scare him off. "Do you think he's gone, then?"

"I'm not sure." He hadn't looked at me once, his eyes glued to the floor. "But he definitely knows I'm officially his enemy. I don't think he'll strike at you in the open anymore. We come as a package deal."

I wrapped my arms around his neck and moved into his chest, holding him and letting him hold me. I'd never felt so safe as I did with this man. Christopher was strong, but Hank didn't see him as a problem at all. But Calloway was different. He was strong and powerful. He was wealthy, with influence. He was the smartest guy I'd ever known. "Thank you."

When he heard the sincerity in my voice, he wrapped his arms around my waist and pulled me closer into him. "You don't need to worry about him anymore, sweetheart. As long as I'm around, he won't touch you." He moved his lips to my hairline and gave me a gentle kiss as his arms tightened around me.

I closed my eyes and rested against his powerful chest, wishing we were home and alone together. Calloway gave me the greatest gift anyone could have ever given me. He gave me back my freedom, gave me back my liberty.

———————

I shut my office door so I could talk to Christopher without anyone eavesdropping. "Hey."

"Hey, how's it going with that caveman? I haven't talked to you in a while and just want to make sure he didn't eat you or something."

He ate me all the time, in fact. "It's been really good, actually."

"Glad to hear that."

"But that doesn't mean I'm not still pissed at you." Christopher and I hadn't talked in a while, and I knew he did that on purpose so I would cool off. But he knew me better than that. I didn't forget easily.

Christopher sighed into the phone. "I'm sorry, okay? But I did what I thought I had to do."

"I specifically told you not to tell Calloway."

His anger flared just the way mine did. "It was

either that or let that psychopath get to you. I honestly believed you would be safer with Calloway than you would ever be with me. I'm sorry you're angry, but that's too damn bad. I made my choice, and I don't regret it. You're my sister, Rome. I've got to protect you —even if I piss you off in the process."

After hearing Christopher defend himself, I couldn't stay angry. Besides, he ended up being right. "You were right about Calloway. He's the only person Hank seems to be afraid of."

"What do you mean?"

"Hank tried to corner me outside the office today. Calloway was with me, and he scared him off with just a look. I've never seen Hank back down from a fight. Actually, he nearly ran. I don't know if this means Hank is gone forever, but I think it's a good sign."

"Hell yeah." Christopher clapped his hands together hard over the line. "Calloway is the fucking man. I told you. I told you that from the beginning, Rome. You're staying there forever. Helps me sleep at night."

"I don't know about forever..." Now that I was living there again, I didn't want to leave. I loved sharing Calloway's bedroom with him. I loved sleeping in that enormous bed with him right beside me. We had a routine every morning before work and every night before bed. I treasured it.

"He told me he gave up everything for you, Rome. Yes, I think this is forever."

"He told you...?"

"I called him the other day," Christopher explained. "Just to check in."

I thought Christopher was pissed at Calloway for lying to me. He obviously got over it. "He hasn't told me he loves me."

"Not with words, no. But he does."

"Why do you think that?" My heart was racing in my chest, the adrenaline flooding my body. There was nothing I wanted more than to tell him I loved him and hear him say it back.

"Are we gossip girls again?"

"Just answer the question."

"Because it's obvious, Rome," he snapped. "The guy is letting you live with him again. He watches every step you take. He's given up Ruin for you. Do I really need to spell it out for you?"

"Then why won't he just tell me?"

"Because words are stupid. They're meaningless. They can be taken back with the snap of a finger. But his actions say everything that needs to be said, Rome. Maybe he's just afraid of intimacy. Maybe he's just afraid to say the words out loud. But he does love you. We both know it."

When I'd told Calloway I loved him, his eyes softened in a way they never had before. Then he'd made sweet love to me on the couch, moving slow and taking his time so we could enjoy each other as much as the sex. I believed he did love me. He just wasn't ready to say it.

———

Calloway came to my office at the end of the day right on time. "Ready to go, sweetheart?" He gave me an endearment right in the middle of the hallway where everyone could hear. But he clearly didn't care.

Since everyone knew I was sleeping with him, I guess a nickname really didn't make a difference at this point. I grabbed my stuff and met him at the door.

He looked down at me like he wanted to kiss me. He eyed my lips with his usual look of intensity, probably wanting to pin me against the wall and fuck me right then and there. I didn't want him to kiss me because we were at work, but if he did, I wouldn't stop him. He eventually pulled away, having made up his mind.

We left the building and took the car back to his place. When we sat in the back seat together, he grabbed my hand and brushed his thumb over my knuckles. His eyes were glued to the window, but he glanced at me from time to time.

We arrived at home then walked inside. The second we were alone together, the electricity filled the air between us. His desires were an open book. I could feel his arousal without even looking at him.

His hands went around my waist, and he moved me into the wall.

Before he could kiss me, I spoke my mind. "I want to please you."

He eyed my lips, his hands still gripping my hips as he held me against the wall.

"You did something amazing for me today. So I want to do something for you."

His hands tightened on my hips, and his look intensified. "You don't owe me anything, sweetheart." He pressed his face against mine then placed a kiss to the corner of my mouth.

"But I want to…" I moved my hands up his chest and undid the buttons of his shirt, popping one by one. I loosened his tie and let it come apart over his chest. "Whatever you want, Calloway. I'll do it this time."

When his eyes darkened, I knew he understood exactly what I was offering.

He chased away my greatest nightmare and gave me back my freedom. He did so much for me without ever asking for anything in return. I knew he had his fantasies, and I could fulfill one—an innocent one.

"You're sure about that, sweetheart?" He stepped closer to me, his chest pressed against mine as he backed me up into the wall.

"Yes...something tame." He knew I didn't want him ever to raise a hand to me, ever to strike me the way Hank did. Whatever it was, it couldn't be violent in any way.

He struggled to say no, to give me the slow and sensual sex he knew I enjoyed. But his entire body wouldn't allow him to do that. It went against his nature, the beast deep inside him.

He unzipped my dress and let it fall to the floor. Next, he went for my bra and panties, stripping me down until I was completely naked with the exception of my heels. He yanked his tie off then forcefully turned me around without warning. He pushed me against the wall, my tits hitting the cold surface. He bound my wrists together and secured them with his silk tie. His lips remained next to my ear, breathing heavily right into my canal. "Last chance."

I was scared, but I was also excited. "I trust you."

He pressed his face against the back of my neck and took a deep breath, his hands pressing against the wall as they shook. Something I said went straight to his core, went straight to his being.

He kissed the back of my neck. "Fuck, sweetheart." He undid his slacks and let them fall to the floor, his boxers dropping around his ankles. Without any warning, he shoved himself inside me, slamming into me without the gentleness he usually showed. He pumped hard and fast, pinning me against the wall while he fucked me like a madman. He gripped my hips and kept me still as he gave me his long length over and over, breathing and grunting. He fucked me harder than he ever had, like he lost his mind to the carnal temptation.

I arched my back and used the wall for balance since my hands were bound behind my back. I felt his arousal, his adrenaline, and fell into the abyss with him. His cock felt enormous like it always did, but the hurt was so damn good.

I'd already begun to scream just a minute into it. My face was pressed against the wall, and my body shook as he thrust into me like he'd never really fucked me before until now. Now that his secret was out in the open, he showed me all his true colors. He showed me just how rough he liked to fuck.

And it felt good.

"Come for me." He pressed his mouth to my ear. "Now."

I was on the verge, so he didn't need to push me.

"Now." He grabbed me by the throat and gripped me hard, his cock stretching me like I was a plaything rather than a woman.

My body responded to his command like it had a mind of its own. I came with a loud groan, feeling my entire body tighten in ecstasy as the wonderful sensation washed over me. Everything felt so good. I was in heaven and hell at the same time. "Calloway…"

He pumped into me a few more times before he released with a quiet groan, his hand still on my throat and his mouth pressed to my ear. He filled me with all of his seed, giving me another deposit of his come.

When he was finished, he rested against me, with the wall for balance. His cock slowly softened inside me, the blood draining and returning to the rest of his body. A gentle kiss was placed on my cheek then my lips, like he was apologizing for the way he'd just fucked me with abandon.

He finally pulled his cock out of me, making me wince once my pussy was barren of his size. "Let's shower." He still spoke with authority, but now he sounded angry—livid. The awesome sex we just had seemed to piss him off more than satisfy him.

But that couldn't be true.

4

CALLOWAY

I let the water wash over me, the warm drops doing nothing to cure the rage that settled deep inside my chest. Like an earthquake, the aftershocks still rocked my body even after the initial explosion had passed.

Rome finally joined me, stepping into the shower and getting her hair soaked under the water. It immediately clung to her neck as it grew heavy. She eyed me with trepidation, knowing something wasn't right. "What is it?"

I was livid with her even though I shouldn't be. "Don't say that to me again."

"Say what?"

"Don't tempt me." I didn't squirt the shampoo into my hair or rub soap on my body. My arms remained by my sides where I knew they would say. "You asked me

57

to give up everything for you, and I have. Don't tempt me with possibilities. Don't remind me of what I'm missing. It'll only make it harder for me."

Her eyes fell, like she hadn't realized her error until now.

"If you want vanilla, I'll give you vanilla. But don't let me even think about the darker flavor that I'm into. Don't play games with me, Rome."

Her eyes remained on the drain in the bottom of the shower, reminding me of the submissive I wished she could be. "I'm sorry. I didn't mean—"

"Well, don't do it again." I squirted shampoo into my hand and massaged my hair, digging my fingernails into my scalp. I didn't look at Rome, existing in my own bubble of frustration.

Her somber expression quickly faded away, replaced by a fiery one. "Calloway, I apologized. No need to talk to me that way."

I tilted my head under the water and let the suds drip down my body. The day had been a nightmare. Looking at Hank made me want to commit murder. And then I got a taste of dominance, a taste of the life I used to live. That short experience reminded me of everything I was missing. The fact that I could have it made me momentarily angry. And then it pissed me off that I caved to her, let her break me.

"I wasn't thinking, Calloway. You've done so much for me, and I just wanted to do something for you. That's all."

I knew my rage was misplaced. The dominant side of me came out, unleashed and powerful. Now that he was out, it was difficult to control him. But I knew I had to box him back up, to return him to the dark depths where he belonged.

I should apologize for the vicious way I spoke to her, but I couldn't bring myself to do that. Instead, I closed the gap between us and placed my hands on each of her cheeks. I pressed my forehead against hers and held her under the water, apologizing with affection rather than words.

Her hands moved around my wrists, and she closed her eyes, enjoying the paramount electricity that ran through us. It made my body hum to life, to feel the natural connection that formed between us the second I saw her in that bar. I could feel the solid touch of her black ring, the ring she agreed to wear so I could fully possess her. We both agreed she was mine, but that didn't seem to be enough for me.

I moved my lips to her forehead and placed a gentle kiss there, feeling myself finally calm down now that I was this close to her. The better version of myself, the generous humanitarian, was back once more. I shut out the dark side of me, the evil one. "I'm sorry."

When she was wet under the shower, she looked beautiful. Her makeup ran down her cheeks, the mascara dripping, but the sight was still extraordinary. Her strength and power emitted from her in small waves. She let her guard down around me, but she was still the strong woman I'd come to worship. "It's okay, Calloway."

---

Was Hank really gone?

That sounded too good to be true.

The second he looked at me, he'd seemed utterly terrified. Like a little boy running back to his mommy, he took off at nearly a dead run. He realized Rome was no longer a vulnerable woman. She had a Roman soldier for a bodyguard, a man that made the soldier in *300* look pitiful.

He couldn't fuck with me.

If that was the solution to everything, then great. But I feared that was too simple, too easy. If only Rome had told me the truth sooner, I could have chased away her demon so easily. Even if he was a difficult opponent, I still could have made this problem go away from her.

When she slept in my arms every night, I knew she felt safe. When I took her everywhere, I knew she appreciated having me by her side. She wasn't the kind of woman to show fear. In fact, she usually objected to my protection. She had no problem staying in a sketchy apartment or taking the subway every day to work. But now that she was really afraid of Hank, she accepted my help without objection.

In fact, she wanted it.

And that made me want her more. I wanted her to want me, to need me. It made me feel more like a man. She was such a woman, the curvy one who didn't put up with bullshit, and having a strong woman rely on me just made me hard. I liked being her champion, her protector.

Hot as hell.

We had dinner together then sat in the living room together and watched TV. Like always, Rome worked on paperwork from the office as she sat beside me, the hardest working person at the company. She took on extra projects without getting paid for the extra work, and she lightened the load of her colleagues.

But now that they knew she was sleeping with me, all that hard work meant nothing to them. They hated her, regardless.

I rested my arm over the back of the couch and

explored her hair with my fingertips, feeling the soft strands move against my callused skin. Instead of watching the TV, I watched her. She had the most elegant jaw, hard with strength but soft like a goddess. Her lips were always magnetic, attracting my lips like a bee to a flower. She was so beautiful, it hurt me sometimes.

She took her eyes away from her work and glanced at me. She wore a light smile on her lips, playful and serious at the same time. "Hmm?"

"Hmm, what?"

"Why are you staring at me?"

"Because you're beautiful." I leaned toward her and placed a kiss on her neck, feeling the warm skin against my lips.

She immediately tensed underneath me, her neck craning to the side to give me more room. Her body reactions told me everything I needed to know. I knew when she wanted me. And I knew when she really wanted me.

I pulled her paperwork off her lap and pushed it onto the floor, hearing the papers scatter once they hit the hardwood. My body guided hers down to the couch, making her back hit the cushions and her head the armrest.

She was in one of my oversized t-shirts, so getting

her panties off was easy. I yanked my sweats and boxers over my ass and to my thighs so my cock could come free. He was already hard and anxious for the woman who stole his obsession.

Her legs moved around my waist until her ankles hooked together at my lower back. With enthusiasm, she wrapped her arms around my neck and dug her fingers into my hair. She breathed against my mouth before she kissed me, her lips trembling. "I want you inside me…" She pulled me closer to her with her legs, suddenly impatient for my cock.

I loved her fire, her desperation. She'd been hot for me since that night we formally met at the charity event. She wanted to invite me inside and give me her virginity then and there, but somehow managed to stop herself. Now she was ready to go at a moment's notice, just as eager for me as I was for her.

Even if the sex wasn't rough like I preferred, it still satisfied me. I loved the moment right before I entered her, seeing arousal in her eyes. She wanted my cock, and she was practically begging for it. The fact that I was the only man ever to have been inside her just made it better. She loved sex because of me—and only me.

I rubbed my cock against her folds, immediately becoming drenched in her wetness. I automatically groaned at the touch, the smell of sex entering my nose at the same time. My cock was hard and throbbing, excited like I'd never fucked her before. "You want my cock, sweetheart?"

She kissed me and inserted her tongue into my mouth, her passion amplified. "I want you." She gripped my ass and pulled me into her, silently begging for my cock. "Make love to me."

When my woman asked for it, I didn't make her wait. I grabbed my base and pressed my tip inside her, greeted by her wetness. I gently pushed inside her, taking her slowly unlike earlier in the day. I slid through her slickness and her tightness, finally inserting my length completely inside her. "Fuck, Rome." I dug one hand into her hair, getting a tight grip on her so she wouldn't slip away. She was my woman, and I wanted to adore her the way she deserved. Anytime I was inside her, I was her at her mercy. I'd do anything she asked—then and there. Her pussy was more addictive than cocaine.

She grabbed my shirt and yanked it over my head so she could feel my chest with her bare hands. She dragged her nails over my skin slightly, nearly scratching me. She rocked her hips with me, taking my cock just as I was giving it to her. Her sexy moans accompanied the noises our bodies made as we moved together. Her hair was spread out over the armrest, scattered and messy. Her eyes shone with their usual fire, her mouth slightly parted against mine.

Fuck, I already wanted to come.

She touched me everywhere, worshiping me like I was the only man she adored. Her pussy seemed to get tighter the longer we moved together. My cock had marked her body as its own, and he understood every little feature. Her shirt was still on so her tits were covered, but something about being clothed turned me on. We couldn't wait long enough to get naked. We just wanted to feel each other as fast as possible.

She couldn't kiss me anymore because she was moaning, her pants hitting me in the face. Her pussy got tighter and tighter, constricting around my throbbing cock as she approached her climax.

Now I really wanted to come. Making Rome come just made feel more alive.

She dragged her nails down my back as she came, moaning directly into my mouth as she rode the exquisite high I gave her. Her nails dug deeper, and she grew tighter around me as the feelings washed over her. It seemed to stretch on forever, and I enjoyed all the expressions she made, the way her face lit up with orgasmic euphoria.

She laid her head back and arched her back underneath me, enjoying the final sensations that formed between her legs. She breathed through the crescendo, her nails slowly relaxing and releasing from where they were lodged in my skin.

Now I wanted to release inside her, to fill her with so much come that it wouldn't all fit. I've never been so obsessed, so committed with another woman. The affection and the attraction just made the sex a million times better. Without the whips and chains, it was still thoroughly enjoyable.

She looked into my eyes with a sex-crazed look on her face, still high from the climax she'd just received. Her hands moved to my shoulders before her fingers dug into my hair once more. "I love you, Calloway." She said it with a strong voice, her resolution undeniable. Her eyes were glued to mine as she spoke, the words rolling off her tongue like she'd said them a million times.

I loved hearing her say that even though I couldn't say it back. Knowing she was head over heels for me made me feel like the luckiest man in the world. I had the love of the most beautiful woman I'd ever seen. In that very moment, she was writhing underneath me, prepared to take all of my come with eagerness.

"Say it again."

She cupped my face and kissed the corner of my mouth. "I love you, Calloway."

Her words hit a trigger deep inside me, and I came with a loud grunt. I shoved my cock as deep inside her as I could go and gave her all of my come, wanting her to take every single drop and keep it. I'd never gotten off to such a romantic thing, but her commitment to me was utterly sexy. I loved having her devotion, feeling like I'd done something right to deserve it.

I dumped all of my seed inside her then kissed her on the mouth, my cock slowly softening inside her stuffed pussy. I felt my come push around my length as my dick slowly became smaller and smaller. Something about my come sitting inside her turned me on like nothing else. It made me feel like I'd claimed her in a way no one else ever had.

"Don't pull out." She grabbed my ass and kept me positioned at her entrance.

I stared at the sex heathen underneath me, seeing her want me more than she ever had before. I suspected it had something to do with the fact that I'd chased away her notorious enemy. She felt indebted to me for fixing a problem no one else could solve for her. The police failed her, and Christopher was powerless to do anything. I was the one man who could set her free — and now she worshiped me even more. "I'm not going anywhere, sweetheart."

I lay beside her in bed, spooning her from behind. Her ass was pressed into my crotch, but I'd made love to her enough times that evening that just holding her was enough. My face was pressed against the back of her neck, and I inhaled her scent as I slowly drifted off to sleep. I counted her breaths as I cherished the moment, remembering exactly what it was like to sleep alone.

I was miserable.

There was no greater feeling in the world than having her in my arms again. Not wondering if she was wrapped in the arms of another man. Every time her back rose from a breath, it pressed against my chest. Something about that sensation made me feel more relaxed than anything else.

I used to be unable to sleep with anyone in the house. Then Rome walked into my life and changed everything. Now I couldn't sleep well unless she was right beside me, my arms protective barriers around her. I wanted her under my nose at all times, not just to protect her, but just to be with her constantly. I'd never been that way before.

I preferred solitude.

I could tell she was dead asleep because of her breathing pattern. Whenever her head hit the pillow, she went out like a light. The only time she struggled was when she had that nightmare a few nights ago. But I suspected she wouldn't have another one since I'd scared the shit out of Hank.

My phone went off on my nightstand, ringing loudly even though it was almost eleven.

What the fuck?

Rome immediately stirred at the sound, the noise impossible not to notice.

I spotted Jackson's name on the screen before I answered. "What?"

"Uh, hello to you too."

"It's eleven." No one called anyone at this time unless it was important.

"So? Are you an old married couple now? You used to go to bed at two at the earliest."

The room was quiet and his voice was loud through the phone, so Rome could hear everything. "Did you need something, Jackson?"

"Yeah, I'm having some problems at Ruin. Can you come by?"

"Tonight?" I asked incredulously.

"Yes. Tonight." He didn't insult me as much as he normally would, probably because he needed something. "You coming or what?"

The time of night made no difference to me. But

Rome was a problem. I couldn't leave her here alone, even though it was unlikely Hank would do anything. He probably gave up his stalker tendencies when he realized I could crush his skull with my bare hand. I debated what to do in my head.

"Hello?" he asked with an irritated voice.

"I'm thinking, idiot."

"Think harder."

I didn't want Ruin to change even though I was no longer a part of it. I wanted it to remain as perfect as it was. "I'll be there in fifteen minutes."

"Awesome. See you in a bit." He hung up.

Rome continued to lie there like nothing happened, caring more about sleep than my conversation with my brother.

"Sweetheart, let's get dressed." I kissed her bare shoulder in apology, wishing I didn't have to disturb her beauty rest.

"Why?" she asked with a sleepy moan.

"We need to stop by Ruin."

"You can go without me." She hugged the pillow tighter.

"Actually, I can't." I brushed my lips against her shoulder again. "I don't want to leave you here alone in the middle of the night."

"I'm sure I'll be fine, Calloway."

"I'd rather not take the chance." To get her ass into gear, I yanked the sheets off her and let the cold air hit her. "Come on. You can sit in the office while I take care of business. You can even sleep if you want to."

She groaned in response.

"This is what's gonna happen." I moved on top of her and pressed my face close to hers. "Get your ass up, or I'll carry you. What's it gonna be?"

She hooked her legs around my waist. "How about we make love and go back to sleep instead?"

I groaned quietly under my breath, hating the brilliant tactic she just used. If she ever wanted to keep me under her thumb, all she had to offer was sex. Like a mindless idiot, I turned into a sex-crazed man who was obsessed with his woman. "As tempting as that sounds, I'm needed elsewhere."

She pouted her lips in protest. "Hank isn't going to bother me." She dragged her hands down my chest. "My big, sexy man chased him off."

I closed my eyes and released another frustrated sigh. "I know what you're doing."

"Then let me do it," she countered. "Make love to me then go to Ruin."

My cock knew what he wanted, but my need to protect her came first. "Get your ass up. Don't make me

71

ask you again." This time, I left the bed altogether so I wouldn't be tempted to sink between her legs.

She knew her tactics weren't going to work, so she sighed and got out of bed. "Just let me put on my makeup and find something to wear."

"You don't need makeup." I loved the way she looked first thing in the morning, with a fresh face and rested eyes. I took her features in completely, seeing past the eyeliner and foundation she wore to work. In either scenario, she looked incredible. But she was one of the few women who didn't need any help in the beauty department. "I'll only be there for twenty minutes." It hit me then that I was taking Rome to Ruin, to the place that contained my essence. She would see firsthand the kind of shit I used to be into—was still into.

"Then why do you need me to come at all?"

I walked up to her and almost grabbed her by the neck, the way I used to touch Isabella. The disobedience and the questions rubbed me the wrong way, antagonized me to my core. But I kept my hand steady, respecting Rome's wishes. "You know why."

The bouncer took one look at me and stepped aside. "Good evening, Mr. Owens."

"Hey, Charles." I fist-bumped him then grabbed Rome's hand, keeping her by my side. She wore the sub ring so every Dom in this place would know and respect that she was mine. But I wanted to keep her close anyway.

The music blared over the speakers, and the lighting was dim so people could be engulfed in the shadows. Some women were dressed in skintight leather. Some women were topless, their nipples pierced with a chain that connected their tits. Men walked their subs with leashes around their necks, yanking on the chain when their women didn't keep up with them.

My arm moved around Rome's waist, and I guided her through the throng of chaos and to the second level. She saw so many things at once, an in-depth view of the underworld. It was the kind of thing you couldn't forget.

I pulled her past the bar and to one of the hallways that contained the private rooms. She was pressed right into my side, and there was no mistaking she was my property. I didn't want the other men even to look at her. Hopefully, there would be no repercussions for bringing her here tonight. She could be reminded why she left me to begin with and take off again. Now that

Hank wasn't a problem, there was nothing stopping her.

But I wouldn't let her go.

I couldn't.

I opened the office door and entered the room where I used to sit and think all the time. Isabella used to kneel in front of my desk until I was finished with my work. Then she and I had our fun afterward.

Jackson was there, and it was obvious he was leaving his mark on the place. Papers were scattered everywhere, and my desk was completely rearranged. A woman lay on one of the couches against the wall, wearing a black corset with leather pants. She stretched her arms above her head, her hair cascading across the cushions.

"I'm here." I released Rome's hand once I was in front of the desk. "Take a seat, sweetheart."

She eyed the woman on the other couch like I'd just asked her to join her.

I patted the leather chair in front of the desk. "I'll just be a few minutes."

She lowered herself then crossed her legs, trying not to stare at anyone with too much focus.

Jackson eyed her then looked at me with a grin.

I shot him a glare, warning him it would be stupid to make an idiotic comment right now.

Jackson didn't call my bluff. "I've been having problems with the place. I asked around, but I couldn't figure it out on my own. So thanks for coming down."

"Let's just not make it a habit, alright?"

"You dropped this in my lap, asshole. I had no time to prepare."

"You've been working with me for twenty years," I snapped. "You've had plenty of time to prepare. It's not my fault you don't listen. Now let's get this shit over with."

"So you can go back to your boring, vanilla life?"

I warned him with just my expression. "You want me to walk out right now?"

He rolled his eyes and came around the desk. "Maybe you've given me Ruin, but we both know you'll always be attached to this place." He headed to the door. "Come on, follow me."

I gave Rome a final look, hoping I wouldn't see disappointment or resentment.

Her expression was nonexistent, blank like a wall. Whatever thoughts she had, she was determined to keep them from me.

---

It took us about thirty minutes to address all the

problems. Jackson hadn't understood how much I really did around Ruin. The instant I was gone, he realized he didn't know how to handle all the electronics of this place, how to control the light show, and other things that seemed insignificant to him but really made an impact on the club.

"How's it going with Vanilla?" he asked when we were finished.

"No complaints."

We stood on the top level near the private rooms, on the opposite side of where my old office was. "Really?" Jackson asked incredulously. "It's been a month, and you don't have any complaints?"

Yes, I missed being a Dom. Settling for just being her boyfriend was difficult at times. But most of the time, I was happy. When I compared my life with her now to what it was when I lost her, I knew I made the right decision. "Some days are worse than others." When she'd opened the cage and let my Dom side come out, just for a moment, it was nearly impossible to get him back inside.

"You think you can do this forever?" People passed us in the hallway, couples heading off to a VIP playroom.

"I don't know." Maybe it would become routine in time. Maybe I would do it for so long that I would change. Maybe one day, my violent tendencies would fade away.

"I've kinda been wondering if you're gonna come back…" He crossed his arms over his chest, his head slightly bowed.

"Do you want me to come back?"

After a long pause, he shrugged. "I guess running Ruin isn't as cool as I thought it would be. Requires a lot of work. You know me, I like to fuck around and take my check. You're a better owner than I'll ever be. But we both already knew that."

I couldn't come back, even if Jackson asked me to. The temptation was just too much. I couldn't leave Rome alone in my bed while I snuck off to the underworld. It would just try my patience, break my exterior. "You'll catch on, Jackson."

"Yeah, but I don't want to. So, this thing with Rome is permanent? I've just got to accept it?"

"Yeah." I still couldn't picture myself getting married. I couldn't even tell her I loved her. I gave up my dominance for her, but there were other things I couldn't budge on. Maybe it would take more time. Or maybe it just wouldn't happen.

"Can't you just keep running Ruin and go back home to her?"

I shook my head. "You know that will be too difficult for me."

"It's not like you were cheating on Isabella while you were here."

It wasn't the same thing, and he knew it. "If we're done here, I should be getting home."

When Jackson didn't move, it was clear the conversation wasn't over. "Isabella has been better."

I wanted to say I didn't care, but I did. I didn't feel anything for her, but I certainly didn't want her to be miserable. I spent a year of my life with her. I wanted her to have something passionate with another man, whether it was a Dom or a regular man. "Good for her."

"But she still asks about you a lot. When I told you were walking away from Ruin, she was disappointed."

"Life goes on, right?" Even if Jackson wasn't finished with this conversation, I was. I turned and walked back to the office.

Jackson caved and followed me. "How's that psychopath? Has he left Rome alone yet?"

"I think I chased him off. He obviously values his life and made the right decision to walk away."

"If he gives you guys any trouble, let me know. I wouldn't mind killing him with my bare hands."

Jackson could be an enigma sometimes. He could

piss me off like crazy, but when it came to the things that mattered, he was there. "Thanks." We just crossed the bridge to the other side when Isabella appeared. Like she had a radar and could track my every movement, she always seemed to pinpoint my location.

Judging by the surprise on her face, she wasn't expecting to see me. She stared at me with her mocha-colored eyes, taking me in just the way she used to. There was still longing there, memories of the intense relationship we used to have.

I was so focused on her face, her jet-black hair, that I didn't notice the man behind her. He caught up to her and circled his arm around her waist, oblivious to the eye contact Isabella and I shared.

She and I passed each other, her shoulder nearly brushing against my arm. It was just an instant, and then it was over. I kept walking, and so did she. I was glad to see her with someone else, to see her beautiful face instead of a waterfall of tears.

It finally took the guilt off my shoulders.

I hoped that was finally the end for her and me, that she accepted the fact that I was devoted to another woman for good. There was no possibility of us getting back together. I was happy where I was—with the woman I was obsessed with.

When Isabella was out of earshot, Jackson spoke. "You took that well."

"I don't care if she's seeing someone else."

"I know that. But they're on their way to a playroom. I'm sure that brings up memories for you."

I'd never forget the way a whip felt in my grasp. I'd never forget the way a woman's ass reddened under the bite of my leather belt. Zip ties, chains, and handcuffs all flooded my mind, the arousal accompanying it.

I pushed the thought out of my brain, refusing to let them in. "I'm fine."

---

Rome and I didn't speak on the way home.

I drove through the nearly empty streets and back to my house at the edge of the city. She was silent from her side of the car, either because she was upset or because she was exhausted. Normally, I could read her pretty well, but right now, I was totally clueless. Without looking into those stunning green eyes, the portal to her soul, I was blind.

I pulled into the garage, and we walked into the dark house. We'd been gone for an hour and a half, so we would both be tired at work in a couple of hours.

But I'd rather deal with her being a little tired than being kidnapped by that psychopath.

We went upstairs and removed our clothes so we could get back into bed. My thoughts kept switching to the depraved things I wanted to do to Rome. I continued to picture her hands tied behind her back with her ass in the air, her ankles chained together by shackles. I imagined her suspended from the ceiling with her legs wrapped around my waist. I pictured spanking her with my palm until both of her cheeks were red.

Now I was as hard as stone.

I didn't want to cuddle with her because she would know how aroused I was, and she would probably figure out what contributed to my hard-on. It was best to keep my distance and try to think of something else.

Rome turned on her side away from me, her knees pulled toward her chest. When she didn't show me any affection, I knew something was wrong.

But I didn't want to talk about it, not when I didn't have a good argument. It was best to say nothing and hope she would cool off in the morning. There was nothing to say that hadn't been said already anyway.

## 5

## ROME

We did our usual routine in the morning. We got ready and headed to work together at the same time. Usually, we held hands during the drive, Calloway's large thumb moving over my knuckles. But today, we didn't share any affection.

When we arrived at work, we walked past the rest of the staff without our usual dramatic appearance. We walked side by side, our arms nearly touching. But to everyone else, that was pretty much us fucking.

Calloway walked me to my office even though it was unnecessary. Even when Hank was a bigger threat, it still didn't need to happen. But I wasn't in the mood to argue, so I didn't bother fighting it.

He stood in the doorway and stared at me, his blue eyes saying what his lips couldn't. He gave me his typical piercing gaze, apologizing but also standing his ground at the same time. With those powerful shoulders, chiseled physique, and movie-star face, it was difficult not to want him—even after last night.

"I'll see you later." I walked into my office so I wouldn't have to look at him anymore. I wasn't entirely sure what I felt about last night. But whatever it was, it wasn't good.

He followed me inside then wrapped his arm around my waist. He pulled me into his chest and gave me a slow kiss on the lips, not giving a damn if a colleague walked by and spotted the affection.

I wanted to push him off, but my body immediately responded. Right on cue, my lips kissed him back, and my heart fluttered like the wings of a butterfly. My arms rested on his, and I felt his hard-on through his slacks.

He pulled away and looked at me with his intense gaze, clearly wanting to kiss me longer and harder. If he could get away with it, he would have lifted me onto the desk and taken me then and there.

But he made the right decision.

Without saying another word, he walked out and headed to his office.

I leaned against the desk and gripped the edge,

knowing I was going to think about that kiss all day until I got another one.

---

We had a meeting in the conference room during lunch.

And that meant it was one of the rare times I would see Calloway during working hours.

I took a seat with my sandwich and salad, and of course, no one sat beside me until just before the meeting started and there weren't any other chairs to choose from. Bill sat on my right, Alexa on my left.

I didn't get any kind of greeting.

Calloway walked in right at the last minute, waiting until everyone in the office was ready before he made his appearance. He walked to the very head of the table, the chair that everyone knew was reserved for him.

But he didn't take a seat.

He grabbed the remote for the projector and clicked a button. "Good afternoon, everyone. We're going to go over the last quarter because we could make some serious improvements." He clicked the button again and changed the slide. Like a bull that had been released from his cage, he reared his head and seemed angry. Sometimes it was difficult to tell if he was intense and focused or just pissed off.

Either way, he looked sexy as hell.

Instead of listening to what he was saying, I kept fantasizing about him. He looked so sexy in that black suit, his shoulders broad and powerful and his legs muscular and long. If I had to sit there and look at him for an hour, I knew it was impossible not to think about sex.

I was sure every other woman in the room was thinking the same thing.

I pictured myself falling to my knees in front of him, his enormous cock shoved down my throat as he gripped my hair like it was reins of a horse.

I drank some water and forced myself to cool off.

"We're invited to a city-wide charity event taking place at the Plaza next Saturday. This is a work function, and I expect everyone to be there. Each of you will get overtime for the appearance. If you have a conflict, speak to Theresa about it, and we'll see what we can do."

Everyone gathered their things, assuming the meeting was over.

"I'm not done." Calloway's deep voice echoed in the room, making everyone flinch in their seats. His employees respected him and the company he built, and they rarely heard him turn dark like that. I was used to it, but I knew they weren't.

He tossed the remote on the table and placed his hands in his pockets. "I have to say how disappointed I am in all of you for the way you've been treating Rome."

Oh god.

No.

What the hell was he doing?

"Yes, I'm sleeping with her. Yes, she's an employee. But frankly, it's none of your concern. Rome is the hardest worker here. She picks up your slack without expecting a thank you, and we've never been so productive as we have since she came on board. All the improvements we need to make are coming from your negligence, not hers. So instead of ostracizing her like this is a high school lunchroom, I expect each and every one of you to treat her with respect just as you did before we made our relationship public. If you can't do that, I'm more than happy to replace you." He grabbed a stack of folders and dropped it on the table. It made a loud thud once it hit the surface of the wood. "These are all the applications I've gotten—in a month." There had to be hundreds in the pile. "Just so you know."

I was mortified.

He dropped a bomb I had no idea was coming. I just assumed it was going to be a regular quarterly meeting, like the others we'd had in the past. But he took the opportunity to put our relationship on blast.

I was certain he'd just made the situation worse.

I spent the rest of the afternoon in my office, trying to hide from everyone else so they wouldn't see how red my cheeks were. It would take at least a month for everyone to stop talking about it.

Maybe longer than that.

"Hey, Rome." Alexa knocked on my open door before she stepped inside.

Maybe I should have kept my door closed. "Hey, Alexa. How can I help you?" When my colleagues needed something from me, they usually just sent an email. Since they used to come to my office, I knew that was just a tactic to avoid me. It was very rare to speak to someone face-to-face.

"I'm going to the café downstairs. You want anything?" She didn't look at me with that judgmental stare I was used to getting. She'd even personally given it to me a few times.

"Uh…" I couldn't think quickly on my feet, so surprised by the offer. "Yeah, I'll take a black coffee." I didn't even want any coffee, but I just wanted to make this conversation go well. I grabbed my wallet and searched for some cash.

"I got it," she said as she walked out. "You can get me next time."

Now I wasn't sure what was going on. Were people going to change their attitudes just to keep their jobs? Or did they realize they were all being assholes to me? I wasn't sure, but I hoped it was the latter.

---

Calloway came to my office when he was finished with his day. Sometimes he worked later than everyone else because he had more things to do, so I just worked until he arrived at my door.

He leaned against the doorframe and silently announced himself. His presence was powerful enough that I could tell when he was walking down the hallway toward my office. I couldn't hear him, but I could certainly feel him.

Like usual, I organized my things then walked out with him.

Calloway walked with his hands in his pockets and said goodbye to the few people who remained at their desks.

They said goodbye to me too, which was a nice change.

The second we were in the elevator with the doors closed, I spoke my mind. "Are you crazy?"

"Yes." He stared straight ahead of him. "But you already knew that."

"I can't believe you said all of that at the meeting."

"I don't care. I own this company, and I can do whatever the hell I want." He glanced at me, his eyes radiating authority. "If they don't like it, they can get another job. I offer great salaries, full benefits, a ridiculous amount of time for sick and maternity leave, and a pension. So maybe they should appreciate what I've given them and show it by treating you like a human being and not a whore."

I knew he meant well, and that touched my heart. "I just don't want people to hate me even more."

"Again, if they have a problem, they can just leave."

Alexa brought me coffee that afternoon, and Bill said hi to me when I grabbed a muffin from the break room. Instantly, everyone was treating me like I wasn't invisible anymore. They were probably just doing it for show, but it was still a nice change.

He adjusted his cuff links without watching his hands. "I've always shown all of them respect. It's time they did the same for me." The doors opened, and he walked out, looking like a model who just walked onto a runway.

We walked to the car, and his driver took us home. Calloway sat on the opposite side of the car, his legs long and his knees open. His elbow rested on the armrest, and he looked out the window, deep in thought.

The driver rolled down the center partition so he could speak to Calloway. "Mr. Owens, your equipment has been delivered. They just finished setting up everything in the garage."

Calloway kept his eyes out the window. "Thank you, Tom."

The driver rolled up the window again.

I was curious to know what kind of equipment he was referring to, but I wasn't sure if it was nosy for me to ask. I decided not to and hoped Calloway would mention it on his own. Right now, I felt like a long-term visitor. The only reason why I lived with him now and in the past was for protection. He'd never officially asked me to live with him permanently, so I didn't feel like I had the right to ask anything.

We arrived at the house and walked inside. Calloway immediately walked into the garage as he loosened the tie around his neck.

I didn't think it would hurt to follow him.

We opened the door where his Aston Martin sat. He had a two-car garage but only one car, so he had extra room inside. Now there was a treadmill, a few weight machines, and free weights, along with a few work-out benches. It was a personal gym, the equipment all brand-new.

Calloway inspected everything, making sure it was exactly what he ordered. He eyed the free weights then examined the treadmill machine.

"I hope you don't expect me to use any of this." I wasn't an athletic person. I'd rather not eat than exercise. That's what I'd been doing my whole life anyway.

He eyed me without an ounce of playfulness. "I've been abandoning my sessions at the gym. I thought if I had my own work-out room, I could work out while you're in the house. Best of both worlds."

"I think you can go to the gym for an hour and leave me alone." After seeing the way Hank turned into a pussy, I wasn't afraid of him anymore. "Or I could go with you to the gym and walk or something."

He walked back to the door. "This is better anyway. I don't like to be around people." He walked inside and locked the door behind us.

Now that we were alone together, the events from last night came into my mind. Calloway knew I was upset, but he hadn't asked me about it. I didn't bring it up either because I wasn't even sure what I wanted to say.

Calloway stripped off his jacket and tossed it on the armrest. He unbuttoned the top of his shirt and let both ends of his tie stretch down his chest. He inserted his hands in his pockets as he stared at me.

I crossed my arms over my chest and stared back.

"You're mad at me." He didn't phrase it as a question, but it came off that way.

"No. Not mad."

"Then what?" he asked quietly.

I knew what Ruin was, but I'd never seen it with my own eyes. I saw things I could never unsee. "I just... I guess I'm floored by what I saw last night." Christopher told me about the women who voluntarily wanted chains around their necks, but seeing it in person changed everything. Women averted their gaze any time a man who wasn't their Dom drew near. Women were second-class citizens—and they wanted it that way. "I guess it still shocks me that's what you're into... that you want me to be that way."

He held my gaze without blinking, his look hard and unreadable. He looked away then rubbed his chin, his callused fingers touching the scruff that grew along his jawline. When he shaved, he looked clean and sexy.

When he didn't shave, he looked rugged and sexy. He brushed his thumb along his bottom lip before he turned back to me. "I'm not going to apologize for what turns me on. I'm not ashamed of my specific tastes. I'll still tell you it's one of the most beautiful relationships between a man and a woman. I would kill to have that with you—to have your unshakable trust. I would love to dominate you, tie you up and control you. I would love to pin you down and take you whenever I felt like it. I would love your obedience." He closed his eyes as if a wave of emotion swept over him. He couldn't continue speaking until he regained control of his sanity. He opened his eyes again, his jaw clenched hard. "I've given you what you want, so you have no right to judge me. You tell me you love me, but I've done something to prove my profound feelings. I've given up my greatest joy to be with you. That's not a simple phrase. That's a sacrifice. There's not a single woman in the world I would have done that for —except you."

I felt two conflicting emotions at once. It still bothered me that he wanted to do those things to me, that he wanted to make me submit to him. To give up my freedom and enjoy his cruelty was something that unnerved me. It would be a crime against my own sex. But then the words he said afterward made me numb everywhere. He wanted to be with me to the exclusion of everything else—and that meant the world to me.

He watched me as he waited for a reaction, for me to say something.

I didn't ever want to be his sub, but something about his words aroused me. I knew if I ever got on my knees and allowed him to command me, he would be harder than he'd ever been. His chest would expand with heavy breaths, and his intensity would multiply by a million. The idea of turning Calloway on turned me on. But I still wouldn't make the sacrifice. "I don't judge you, Calloway. I've never judged you. I just don't understand."

"You would understand if you tried." His words implied what he meant, that I needed to allow him to be a Dom to truly get what he meant. I'd have to step into the darkness with him, to become a demon just like him.

"I just…I wish I was enough for you."

His eyes softened in remorse. "I never said you weren't, Rome. When I went to Ruin, I wasn't hard at the memory of having a sub. I was hard at the fantasy of having you as my sub, of making you my plaything. You've always been enough for me, sweetheart. I don't want anyone else but you."

I looked to the ground, unable to meet his intense gaze any longer.

"After all this time, I wish you understood that I would never hurt you. That what we would have would be nothing like the abusive relationship you had with that asshole."

"I know it would be different, Calloway. I don't compare you — "

"Then why won't you try with me?"

I should have known this would come up eventually. For the first few weeks, we were happy together. But the truth always had a way of coming back. "Because I don't want to, Calloway." I tried to say it as gently as possible even though he would still be disappointed. "I have no desire to be treated that way. I love it when we make love. I love it when we can't even get our clothes off before we fuck on the dining table. That passion is more than enough for me. I don't want it to change."

"What if we had both?"

"No." I didn't want to fulfill his fantasy of being a weak possession.

"I made a sacrifice for you. And you won't make one for me?" He did a good job of keeping the edge out of his voice, but some of his resentment seeped through.

"I never asked you to make the sacrifice."

"Bullshit."

Fire rushed through my body at a million miles an hour. "I said I didn't want to be your sub, and I walked away. You're the one who said you'd change to make this work. I never asked you to."

"But you didn't give me any other choice."

"It's not the same thing," I argued. "If you miss it so much, why don't you just go back to it? You can find a woman far more beautiful than me to get on her knees and ask to be whipped." The idea of him being with anyone else repulsed me, but I was too angry to control my tongue.

"I can't live without you," he snapped. "And don't act like you didn't know that."

"You never tell me you love me."

His nostrils flared like I'd said something that really pissed him off. His shoulders grew rigid with his fury, and he breathed through the rage, attempting to keep himself under control. Then, out of nowhere, he rushed me.

He dashed to me so quickly I could barely see him move. There was nowhere to go but backward, and my back hit the kitchen counter when I ran out of space. He grabbed me by the hips and threw me onto the counter before he grabbed my panties and ripped them apart. He got his slacks undone and his cock out in record time, shoving himself violently inside me.

I gripped his shoulders and held on as he fucked me on the counter, giving it to me hard, without giving my body a moment to acclimate to his enormous size. He was rougher than he'd ever been before, taking me like an animal.

He grabbed the back of my neck and focused my gaze on his, still thrusting deep inside me. "Because I don't need to say it."

## 6

## CALLOWAY

Rome wasn't going to change her mind.

I needed to accept it and move on.

For the most part, I thought I could do that. The sex satisfied me. There was no other woman I wanted to be with besides her. I didn't have fantasies about other women, and I certainly didn't think about my former lover, Isabella.

But there were moments...of weakness.

Sometimes my thoughts would drift away during the workday, thinking about how Rome would look in my exclusive playroom at Ruin. I would graze the edge of the whip across her delicate skin, making patterns in my movements. And then I would strike without warning, tapping her along her back or her ass.

And also the mound between her legs.

I found myself so aroused that I forced myself to

think about work, something I found innately boring. It usually did the trick and caused my cock to deflate like a popped balloon. After a few minutes of tenderness in my balls, that faded away too.

And I returned to calm.

Rome and I didn't talk about our fight again after we fucked on the kitchen counter. We both took out our rage on one another, fucking to rid the irritation we both felt. I wanted her to change for me, to make a compromise. And she wanted me to be purely vanilla, a man satisfied with straight sex.

We would never meet in the middle.

But since there was no other option, I stayed. I could be with another woman, but that would mean she could be with another man.

And that would certainly make me commit murder.

I worked out vigorously that morning before Rome woke up, going for a long run on the treadmill and then hitting the weights hard. I hadn't been sticking to my routine lately because I was too depressed when Rome left me. Then when she came back to me, I didn't want to leave her unprotected just to hit the gym. Getting a private work-out area in my garage seemed to be the best solution to my problem.

I finished a set then sat on the work-out bench, sweat drenched into my clothes and skin. It felt good to work out again. My body finally got to move and feel those endorphins it missed. In some ways, the intensity reminded me of my sessions with a sub—powerful and challenging.

The garage door opened, and Rome stood there in one of my black t-shirts. My clothes were at least three times too big for her, but the shapeless fabric somehow looked sexy on her—probably because it was just another way for me to possess her. "It's Saturday morning."

"Your point?"

"Who works out on a Saturday morning?" she asked incredulously.

"A man with a beautiful woman to satisfy." I racked the weights then wiped the sweat off my forehead with my shirt.

"Well, you could come upstairs and satisfy me," she said playfully. "And ditch the weights."

"They go hand in hand." If I wanted her to remain just as addicted to me as I was to her, I had to keep myself in shape. My body needed to be chiseled from marble, and my muscles needed to be as strong as concrete. Rome loved my size and strength. She never specifically said it, but I could tell.

"I'm gonna make breakfast. You want anything?"

"Egg whites and wheat toast."

She rolled her eyes. "That's the most boring meal I've ever heard of."

"It's not so bad." I massaged my hands because I'd felt the muscles in my joints tighten when I gripped the metal bars of the weights. "I'm gonna shower. I'll join you in fifteen minutes."

"Okay." She rose on her tiptoes and kissed me on the lips, not caring about all the sweat. She placed her hand against my chest, right over my damp shirt. She didn't seem to care about that either because when she pulled away, a smile was on her lips. "I'd love to watch you work out sometime."

"I'll do it shirtless, then." I went upstairs and showered before I joined her at the kitchen table. My boring meal was covered with foil so it would stay warm. I pulled it off then sipped my coffee.

It was obvious neither one of us was going to mention last night. The conversation wasn't going to go anywhere positive. We'd have to accept each other's position and make the best of it. Neither one of us wanted to walk away, to be with anyone else. Ignoring the elephant in the room was the only option we had.

Rome took a bite of her single slice of French toast and read the newspaper. Black circles were marked around certain listings, like she was looking up something for sale.

I sipped my coffee then narrowed my eyes to what she was doing. "What are you doing?"

"I was just checking the listings to see what's available."

"Listings for what?"

"Apartments."

I was about to take a bite of my toast when I hesitated. She was thinking about moving out? "Why would you be looking at an apartment?" Was this because of the fight we had last night?

"I know I moved in here because of the situation with Hank. Now that he's not a problem, I thought I should leave." She finally looked up from the paper and met my look. She immediately flinched when she saw the fury in my eyes.

"For one, we don't know if he's still a problem. He turned into a pussy when he came face-to-face with me, but maybe his balls will grow some courage. Two, you've lived with me once, and you left when I didn't want you to. Now you're trying to leave again. Being together under one roof is what I want. So you aren't going anywhere."

"I just —"

I snatched the paper and crumpled it with one hand before I set it on the table.

Rome remained calm despite my hostility. "You

asked me to live with you because Hank was a problem. I didn't know if that invitation was still active because—"

"It's always active." I wanted her to sleep with me every night. I wanted to look at her face every morning. I wanted us to be together all the time. If she lived somewhere else, it would just be a waste of rent because she would be here all the time anyway. And I would be worried about her living alone.

"So…you're asking me to move in with you?"

"Obviously."

"Calloway." She gave me a firm look, telling me she was being dead serious. "Are you really asking me that?"

We hadn't even been seeing each other for a year yet, and our relationship wasn't even close to being normal. We waited a month to have sex, but our relationship still progressed at an alarmingly rapid rate. But there wasn't a doubt in my mind that she should be there with me. I didn't want her to live on her own just out of principle. I wanted us to be together —always. "No."

Her eyebrows scrunched together.

"I'm telling you to live with me."

Her eyes softened at the remark, the blush moving into her cheeks. When she showed her vulnerable side, she was somehow more beautiful than when she was angry. She took a deep breath like she was trying to control an emotion circling deep inside her chest. "Good. Because I didn't want to leave anyway." She grabbed the balled-up newspaper then tossed it at my face, being playful.

I let it bounce off my cheek before I smiled. "I'm glad we finally agree on something."

---

The second I woke up the next morning, my cock was throbbing and anxious for release. I barely even opened my eyes before I rolled over and moved on top of Rome, separating her thighs with my knees.

She was still half asleep, but her body reciprocated, her legs easily falling open. She took a deep breath as her eyes opened, taking in my features as she ran her fingers over my body. Her body danced slightly, coming alive now that she knew what was coming.

The tip of my dick found her entrance like he had a mind of his own. I slipped inside and felt the moisture between her legs. I pushed through, feeling the slickness as I sank deep inside her. I held myself up on my elbows, choosing to be lazy on a Sunday morning.

Once I was completely inside her, I pressed my face into her neck and thrust slowly inside her.

She wasn't fully conscious yet, but that made the sex better. We could really feel each other without thinking. All we did was enjoy the touch of one another, the ecstasy for our affection. My cock felt right at home in her tight pussy, the place I'd claimed as mine exclusively.

She pressed her face into my neck as her hands gripped my shoulders. She gently rocked with me but allowed me to do most of the work. It was a lazy fuck, one where we were both getting off but doing the least amount of work at the same time.

I never thought I would enjoy it so much.

There was no foreplay. No dirty talk. Just good sex.

She came in record time, breathing hard into my neck as the sensation ripped through her. She sank her teeth into my skin, biting the muscle as she suppressed her scream. Her throat was still raspy from sleeping all night, so her moans didn't come out like they usually did.

Now I wanted to come.

Her pussy was so wet and tight, and she continued to bite me as she dragged her nails down my shoulders.

I moved my lips to her temple as I gave my final pumps. "I love coming inside you, sweetheart."

"Mmm…" She pulled me deep inside her as she prepared for my release.

That sexy little sound she made caused me to explode. I shoved myself as deep inside her as I could go, dumping my seed and feeling high as I did it. There was nothing that made me feel more like a man—coming inside Rome.

I remained in the same position when I was finished, my face still pressed into her neck. I could smell her natural scent so easily, and I adored it. My cock softened inside her but was in no rush to leave. "Good morning."

"Morning." She sighed and kept her limbs locked around me, having no interest in leaving either.

"I could stay just like this all day."

"Me too…except I have to pee."

I chuckled then kissed her hairline. "Good point." I moved off of her and slowly pulled out, my cock still releasing drops of my seed. When I looked down at her entrance, I could see my come dripping out.

Now I was turned on all over again.

Rome moved her fingers between her legs and touched the area, getting the come stuck to her fingers. She popped them into her mouth and sucked.

Holy fuck.

She gave me a seductive grin before she got out of bed.

I wasn't letting her get away after that. I snatched her by the wrist and yanked her back to the bed. Positioning her diagonally across the bed, I moved on top of her again and shoved my semi-hard cock inside her. I moved through her slickness and the remains of my come, and within minutes, I was hard all over again. "You aren't going anywhere."

---

"Since we don't have any plans today, how about we go see your mom?" Rome set the plates on the table, grilled chicken with rice and vegetables. She sat down like the conversation was casual.

But when it came to my mom, it was never casual.

I hadn't read to my mom in a while. I was too distressed when Rome left me, and when she came back, I was too preoccupied. Every time I went and saw my mother, I hoped things would get easier—but they never did.

When I didn't say anything, Rome looked up from her plate and looked at me.

"I haven't seen her in a while. Been meaning to stop by." I took a bite.

"Then we should go today."

I didn't want to make things complicated, but there was something I needed to say. "I appreciate the offer, but you don't have to come with me. I don't mind going alone."

She eyed me hesitantly, like she was unsure if she'd said the wrong thing. "Would you prefer to go alone?"

"No. I just don't want you to feel obligated." She was my mom, not hers. It wasn't a burden for Rome to carry.

"I don't feel obligated, Calloway," she said quietly. "You don't have to do everything alone. We're in this together, you know. You helped me with Hank when you didn't have to. I want to help you in whatever way I can. My presence seems to help her memory…"

The longer this relationship progressed, the more I realized just how dependent I was. Before Rome came into my life, I wasn't attached to anyone or anything. I alone and free, but I was okay with that. But the instant I looked at Rome, I felt something. She turned out to be a woman I could never walk away from. The affection, the closeness, everything was nice. Now I was addicted to it. "Okay. We'll go after we're done eating."

With the same book tucked under my arm, we entered the assisted-living facility and greeted my mother's nurse. She always remembered me since I'd been coming there for years. She knew a lot about my life, about my job, and even my younger brother, Jackson. But it didn't make up for the fact that my mother didn't even remember my face.

We walked to my mother's room, a small one-bedroom apartment with a living room, a kitchen, and a single bedroom down the hallway. It was a nice place with plenty of room for a single person, and the balcony was the best part. It cost me an arm and a leg to keep her here, especially since Jackson refused to contribute. But it was worth it to know she was in a good place.

My mom was on the patio in her rocking chair, like always. When she was well, she used to do the exact same thing. Any excuse to be outside was a good excuse. She liked to spend her time gardening or just sipping a glass of lemonade as she watched the neighborhood kids go by on their bikes.

I examined her features the moment I stepped outside, seeing my eyes in her face. Even without her memory, she possessed the same grace. Her outfits always had to be beautiful and wrinkle-free, and the jewelry she wore was very specific. She had no one to impress, but her need to look nice was one of principle.

Like every other time I saw her, I introduced myself. "I'm Calloway. I'm from Humanitarians United, and I've come to read to you." I extended my hand.

She eyed it for a moment, as if she wasn't sure if she should touch me. Then she placed her hand in mine and gave it a gentle squeeze. "It's nice to meet you, Calloway. Please sit down."

I stepped aside and allowed Rome to greet her next.

My mom stared at her hard, a flash of recognition coming over her face. "Do I know you from somewhere, dear?"

I shouldn't be jealous that my mom remembered Rome better than she remembered me. I should only feel hopeful that there was a possibility that my mom could come back from this, that she could remember some events of her life—including me.

"I came to read to you a while ago." Rome placed her hand over my mother's, her affection warm. "That must be why you recognize me." She leaned down and hugged my mom, wrapping her arms around her.

My mom softened at the touch and returned the embrace, like she was greeting a daughter. "Aren't you sweet?"

Rome sat in the chair beside me, still wearing that gorgeous smile. Not only was she beautiful, but she had this amazing quality that drew everyone's attention.

Something about her made everyone obsessed, wanting to know more about her and be with her constantly. She obviously had some kind of special ability because she changed me—a Dom.

"How's your day going?" Rome crossed her legs and tucked her hair behind her ear.

"It's going," Mom said with a sigh. "I had a difficult morning…couldn't remember where I was or how I got here. It's just one of those days."

I couldn't imagine how that would feel. Every morning, my mother woke up with a blank memory. She didn't remember her family or her friends. She woke up in a place she'd never seen before. Her nurse told me some days were difficult —and others were extremely difficult. "You look nice today, Theresa." It was strange to call her by her first name instead of Mom. Even though I was a grown man, I still preferred to address her as my mother. She was the woman who raised me, after all.

"Thank you…" She searched my face as she tried to recall my name.

"Calloway." I hid my hurt with a smile.

"Calloway…that's a nice name."

That was the twentieth time I'd hear her say that. "Thanks. My mother had good taste."

Rome moved her hand to my knee and gave it a squeeze.

"Are the two of you married?" Mom asked.

"No," I answered. "We're dating."

"You two would make beautiful children," she said, wearing her graceful smile.

"Thanks," Rome said. "Maybe someday."

I couldn't picture myself being a father. I was too fucked up in the head. But if Rome wrapped me any tighter around her finger, who knows what I would do. She practically had magical powers. "Would you like me to read to you?"

"Maybe later," she said. "I want to know more about you. You work where?"

"Humanitarians United," I explained. "It's a nonprofit geared toward helping those in need in the state of New York."

"Sounds like a great program," she whispered. "You volunteer?"

"I work there," I explained. "Employees get a competitive salary. Any extra cash goes back into the program to help those in need."

"That's amazing," she said. "If I had money, I'd give you a donation...but I don't think I have any money." Her eyes trailed away, and she tried to quantify her wealth. She never worked a day in her life because my parents got married very young. But she couldn't remember any of that.

I felt terrible for her. "Don't worry about it. The company is doing really well right now."

"Is that how you both met?" she asked.

I couldn't tell my mother the story of how I met Rome. No one would ever understand. "Yeah."

"That's wonderful," Mom said. "Some people say you shouldn't date someone you work with, but I think that's a great idea. Where else are you going to meet someone?"

In a bar where a woman walks up to you and slaps you.

Mom asked Rome a few other questions about Humanitarians United. The two of them got along well, and I could tell that my mom would love her if she could actually remember her. She would be the ideal daughter-in-law. It was a shame my mother wouldn't remember either one us of the following morning.

Sometimes, I wondered why I put myself through this. Every time I looked at the glaze of confusion in her eyes, my heart broke. Every time I looked at the blank expression on her face, I felt disappointed. And every time I left, I felt like I didn't accomplish a damn thing.

So why keep doing it?

The doctors said it would only get worse from here

on out. There was no possibility of improvement, even with new research. But I hated the idea of my mother being completely alone with no one to visit her. She didn't remember it anyway, but I still wanted to be there for her. I knew she would be there for me if the situations were reversed.

Rome seemed to know I was struggling in my silence because she placed her hand on mine and gave me a look of remorse. She gave my fingertips a gentle squeeze, telling me she was there for me always.

I gave her a slight nod, my poor attempt at showing my appreciation.

Dr. Niles sat behind his desk with my mother's chart in his hand. "How are you today, Mr. Owens?"

I felt like shit. What was new? "Good. You?" Rome sat beside me in the other armchair. She had been planning on waiting outside, but I told her she belonged inside that room with me. I didn't have any secrets from her—not anymore.

"Great." He flipped through my mom's chart before he interlocked his fingers together on the desk. "I've been reviewing your mother's status, and she's in good shape. Strong reflexes, great speech patterns, and her lab results look excellent. Your mother is very healthy."

Other than the fact that she'd completely lost her mind. "Good to know. What about her memory? Can I expect it to get worse?" There wasn't much room for her memory to become more impaired, but the brain was intricate. There could be other complications.

He sighed before he answered. "That remains to be seen. But for now, everything seems about the same."

Rome leaned toward me and whispered. "Should you tell him about the last time you visited…?"

Dr. Niles watched our interaction, his eyes narrowed.

The event hadn't slipped my mind. I just didn't want to get my hopes up only to have the doctor tell me it was a fluke.

Dr. Niles grabbed his pen and clicked the tab with his thumb. He pressed the tip to his notebook. "Would you care to discuss this incident?"

Rome gave me a look of encouragement.

I rubbed the back of my neck before I answered. "I came here a few weeks ago, and she thought she recognized me."

"And did she?" Dr. Niles had his gaze glued to my face, intrigued by the story.

"She recognized me from somewhere but couldn't

recall specifically. Then she mentioned Rome…so she remembered her from the previous visit. But when we spoke with her today, she didn't recognize either one of us. I don't know if that means anything. Could just have been a fluke."

Dr. Niles bit his bottom lip as he jotted everything down, scribbling his notes with suppressed enthusiasm. His glasses sat on the bridge of his nose, slowly sliding forward because he kept his head bent for so long. "That's very interesting…"

"Do you think it means anything?"

He finished writing and set the pen down. "Has she ever done this before?"

"No."

"I'd say it's a good sign. Perhaps she can form new memories but can't recall old ones. I think you should visit her every day, if you can, and perhaps that will make a difference. Sometimes a strong stimulus can change the chemical reactions of the brain. How often do you see her now?"

"Once every few weeks." I didn't go as much as I should, and not because I was lazy. It was just too painful sometimes.

"Try to go every day, and see if that changes anything. The brain is like any other muscle in the body. The more you use it, the stronger it is," Dr. Niles said.

"But she doesn't remember her nurse," Rome said. "And she sees her every day."

"But there's no emotional connection there," Dr. Niles explained. "With the two of you, it could be different. Calloway is her son. She does have memories of him, even if she doesn't realize it. They're just buried deep inside."

I could make time to see my mother every day. I had a lot of things to do, but if there was even a small hope that Rome and I could help her, we had to try. "We'll give it a shot."

***

I sat at my desk and pinched the bridge of my nose, ignoring the documents I needed to sign and the flood of emails that were hitting my inbox. I'd been working nonstop since I arrived that morning, and now I needed a mental break. My mother's illness was weighing on my shoulders that afternoon, plus my current conflict with Rome. I wanted more than vanilla, but she wouldn't give it to me. Also, I feared Jackson was letting Ruin go to shit without me there to hold his hand. Hank was still a problem, as far I could tell.

Everything was going to hell.

The only positive event going on at the office was the fact that my employees finally got their shit together and were treating Rome like a human rather than a prostitute. I was glad they took my threat so seriously because I would have fired every single one of them if they continued to behave like assholes.

My secretary's voice came over the intercom. "Mr. Owens, Isabella is here to see you."

I dropped my hand from my nose and stared at the intercom on my desk. I only knew one woman by that name—and she better not be inside this building. I hit my finger against the button. "Isabella what?"

"Not sure, sir. She said she's from Ruin."

Fuck, it was the same Isabella. I knew it wasn't smart to ignore her. Whatever she came down here to say was obviously important. If I didn't give her the attention she wanted, she would get it some other way —by showing up at my home. "Send her in."

"Of course, Mr. Owens."

I didn't get up from my chair because that was too much work on my end. This had something to do with seeing me at Ruin last week. Maybe she still thought there was hope for us to resume that relationship.

I had to squash that fantasy.

The door opened, and Isabella walked inside, head

held high with confidence. She sauntered into the room as she shook her hips, looking like a model on the catwalk rather than a normal person stopping by someone's office. She was in a tight black dress like she'd just left the hottest club in town.

Any man would think she was beautiful. Stunning, even. She really did have amazing features. High cheekbones, full lips, and almond-shaped eyes that made her features even softer. The first time I looked at her, I thought she was one of a kind. It was strange to look at her now and not feel anything, so contradictory. "Is there something I can help you with, Isabella? I hope you aren't looking for a position. My staff is full." I kept the conversation light because she would take it to a dark place the second she took the reins.

She sat in the leather armchair facing my desk. She crossed her long legs and flipped her hair, clearly trying to capture my sexual attention with her beauty. She'd tried this tactic several times, and I wasn't sure why she kept bothering. "I was just in the neighborhood."

My temper was getting more difficult to restrain. "I'm at work, Isabella. I don't have time to keep you company."

She ignored the last thing I said. "Jackson tells me you're still with that plain girl."

"Trust me, she's not plain."

"She's vanilla," she hissed.

"Vanilla, yes. But not plain." There was a big difference. If Rome could keep my attention with vanilla sex, then it was insulting to Isabella who couldn't get me to stick around with whips and chains. "And yes, Rome and I are very happy."

She propped her elbow on the armrest and set her chin above her slender fingertips. "How long is this really going to last, Calloway? You're just going to hurt the poor girl." Her condescension filled the air, like she was superior to Rome.

"A very long time." It was difficult to imagine it ever ending. The month that we were apart, I was insanely depressed. Couldn't remember the last time I was that low. I went through my entire liquor cabinet and had to have Tom restock it because I was too drunk to do it myself. "I hope that's not why you're here. I assumed you moved on from me." I saw her with that man in the hallway. I couldn't be sure, but he seemed like a Dom. Very few men went there who weren't Doms.

"What we had was too great just to forget about."

"I never said we should forget it. Just move on."

She continued to watch me with her almond eyes, her slender neck soft. I remembered the way it used to feel when I grabbed it. "I know you better than anyone,

Calloway. I know exactly what you're into. I know exactly what you need."

"You aren't the only one."

"She doesn't accept you for who you are. She doesn't appreciate you for the man you've become. But I do, Calloway. I understand exactly what you need and can give it to you. Eventually, you're going to hit a wall in this relationship. You're going to realize you can't keep up with all the sissy shit she's into. You're going to break her heart and waste your time in the process. But with me, you could get exactly what you need."

After all this time, she still wouldn't give up. "Out of respect for what we had, I've been patient with you. But my patience is nearly gone. You and I will never be together again, even if Rome was long gone. Do you understand me, Isabella?"

"Yes." She dropped her arm and continued to stare me down. "I understand you so well that I see the future even better than you do. Calloway, you need to tame your dominance if you want this relationship to work. If not, you'll blow up at the most unsuspecting time. I can fix that for you."

Now I didn't have a clue what she was talking about.

"Let me be your sub, Calloway. Give me commands

to obey. Make me submit. Be the Dom that you were meant to be."

I couldn't deny that I missed it. When she asked me to dominate her, I felt a rush of energy soar through my body. Rome wasn't willing to compromise with me, and the one time she allowed me to take control, I nearly lost myself. "I'm committed to Rome."

"I realize that," she said coldly. "But that doesn't mean you can't be a Dom with me. That doesn't mean I can't be on my knees, the perfect sub. If you tell me to kneel, I will. If you tell me to be silent, I will. We can have what we both want—and you can have what you have with Rome."

She wanted me to be a boyfriend to Rome—and a Dom to her. I hated myself for being tempted by the offer, to exercise my need for control in some way. If I had this with Rome, I wouldn't feel any temptation at all. But that was never going to happen for us.

"There doesn't need to be any sex," she said. "Any touching. Just pure domination."

My right hand formed a fist, tight and painful. I kept a stoic expression, but I was coming undone inside. With all the shit I was going through, I needed to let my inner Dom come out. I needed to vent my frustrations and feelings in the best way I knew how. "No." As much as I wanted to say yes, it would be wrong. Rome would see it as an act of betrayal even though she refused to give me what I needed. And I couldn't hurt the woman I was so obsessed with. I couldn't hurt the woman who slept in my bed every night. She meant far too much to me. "That's my final answer. Don't ask me again."

Isabella's eyes moved to my hand on the desk, the one was clenched tightly in a fist. Her gaze lingered for a long time before she met my look again. A small smile crept on to her lips, like she knew something I didn't. "You know where to find me when you change your mind, Cal."

"I won't change my mind, Isabella."

She rose from the chair and walked to the door, sauntering like a model once more. "You say that now. But you're going to crack, Calloway. Eventually."

## 7

## ROME

I finished up my day and had nothing else to do, so I decided to go to Calloway's office. Everyone knew I was dating him, and since they were all finally being nice to me, I decided to just do what I wanted without worrying what they were thinking of me.

I told his secretary I was outside and waited for him to allow me inside. Once she said it was okay, I opened the door and walked in.

Calloway was in a bad mood. I could tell by the darkness in his eyes and the tightness in his jaw. He didn't stand up to greet me like he usually would. He remained behind his desk, annoyance emitting from him in waves.

"Is this a bad time?" I approached him slowly like he was a wild animal.

"You don't need to ask my secretary if you can walk in, Rome. Just come inside."

"You might be in the middle of a meeting."

His look intensified. "It doesn't matter what I'm doing. You're always welcome."

I would consider his words to be sweet if I didn't feel such hostility at the same time.

He watched me with the same cold expression and didn't move toward me.

I knew he was under a lot of stress. He was worried about his mom, about Ruin, about Hank, and everything else under the sun. The only time he seemed to be in a good mood was when we were having sex.

I walked around his desk then stood behind him. My hands dug into his powerful muscles and I massaged him, trying to rub the tension out of his frame. Through his suit, his muscles were even tighter.

When he spoke again, his tone wasn't so harsh. "Did you need something, sweetheart?"

"No." I moved around him then swung one leg over his lap, straddling him and taking a seat. I ran my hands up his chest and noticed the absence of his hard-on. I couldn't remember the last time I was this close to him without feeling his erection. I hoped it would arrive soon enough. "I'm done for the day, so I thought I would hang out in here until you're finished." My arms circled his neck, and I leaned in and pressed my face to his.

His cock hardened underneath me — right on cue.

At least his anger was going away.

"I don't think I'm going to get anything done now..." He gripped my hips then kissed me on the mouth, his kiss hot and seductive. He pulled my bottom lip into his mouth then squeezed my ass through my dress.

Now that things were heating up, I understood the error of my ways. When he kissed me like that, it always led to passionate sex. It was inappropriate for the office, but Calloway wasn't the type of man to care about professional conduct.

He undid his belt and zipper so his cock could be free. My dress was yanked up, and my panties were pulled to the side. He adjusted my hips and pulled me onto his length, making me slide down until I reached his balls. He pressed his face into my neck and kissed me, his chest rising with the deep breath he took. "Fuck yeah..." His hands returned to my ass, and he guided my hips in just the right way, making me sheathe his length over and over.

The second he was inside me, I forgot about the rules we were breaking and what the consequences would be if someone walked inside. I watched the desire take over his face, the intensity grow in his eyes, and I was lost.

He nicked my collarbone with his teeth then nibbled on my earlobe, his breath warm and seductive. He touched me everywhere before his hand migrated to the area between my legs. He rubbed my clit aggressively, giving me more pleasure than I needed.

I bit my lip so I would remain quiet. His secretary was right outside his door, and I didn't want to embarrass us both for all eternity. But with every touch and every kiss, he was making it impossible for me to stay quiet. I was used to the luxury of privacy, of being able to scream as loud as I wanted when he made me come.

"Come for me, sweetheart." He spoke into my ear, his cock thrusting deep inside me.

I buried my face into his neck and dug my nails into his fine suit. The climax rocked through me so hard it was practically painful. I bit his shoulder as I stifled my moans, feeling my pussy drench his throbbing cock.

"Sweetheart..." He pumped into me a few more times before he found his own release. He was silent, unlike me. He exerted his tension by gripping me tighter, holding on to me so tightly he nearly squeezed the air out of my lungs. His cock continued to move inside me, slowly coming to a stop as he finished giving me all of his come.

I didn't want to move because I was comfortable against his chest, his cock softening inside me. "Looks like I can't come in here anymore."

He brushed a kiss against my hairline. "No. Now I want you in here every day."

---

*I haven't seen you in, like, a million years.* Christopher's message popped up on my phone.

*Sounds like you miss me.*

*Nope. Never said such a thing.*

*Then why are you texting me?*

*Geez, just wanted to see if you wanted to get dinner.*

I sat in the back seat of the car with a smile on my face. *So you do miss me. I knew it.*

*Hell no. So, are we doing this or not?*

I chuckled because Christopher wasn't nearly as sly as he made himself out to be. *Sure. I can meet you in fifteen minutes.*

*I'll swing by the house and pick you up.*

Christopher never offered anything like that, and I knew it was because he was still worried about me. Hank hadn't made a single appearance in weeks. I was pretty certain he was no longer a problem. But I didn't tell Christopher otherwise because Calloway would just bring me there anyway if Christopher didn't escort me. I had to pick one or the other. *Okay.*

Calloway looked out the window and didn't ask who I was texting. He was the jealous type, but he never went through my things or questioned what I was doing. I appreciated that respect, and I gave the respect back to him. "Christopher is going to be at the house in fifteen minutes. Wants to take me to dinner."

"Did he mean to text someone else?" he teased.

I rolled my eyes. "He misses me. I can tell."

"Or he just wants something."

"I doubt it. Christopher isn't really the type of person to ask for anything."

"Wow. Then maybe he actually does like you. Fooled me."

I smacked his forearm playfully. "Shut up."

He chuckled then grabbed my thigh, his knuckles pronounced and muscular. He gave me a sexy squeeze, implying what he could with his hands if I stayed in for the night. "How long will you be gone?"

"I don't know. Depends on Christopher's tolerance."

He laughed. "Then you'll be home in an hour, tops."

I smacked his arm again.

"Long time, no see." He looked me up and down. "But you're still hideous, so I guess some things never change."

I rolled my eyes. "You're paying for dinner now."

"Fine with me. I was gonna treat you anyway." He turned to Calloway and shook his head. "You doing okay with this monster living in your house?"

"She pays her way by cooking, so she's fine," Calloway answered.

And fucking. But I wasn't dumb enough to say that to my brother. "We'll be back later. See ya." I immediately turned toward the door.

Calloway grabbed me by the elbow and yanked me back into his chest, obviously not caring if my brother had an opinion about it. He crushed his mouth to mine and laid a kiss on me, the kind that said he'd be waiting to finish it until I came home. He smacked my ass and turned away. "Good luck, Christopher."

"You're acting like this is my first rodeo." Christopher walked out with me, and we headed up the road side by side. The weather had improved since winter passed. Now springtime filled the air, blossoms blooming on tree branches. Christopher wore a light jacket on his slender frame. "You want to go to that Italian place you like?"

"You remember what places I like?"

"Come on, it's not like we're never met."

"But you never listen to anything I say."

He shrugged. "Maybe I listen more than you realize."

We arrived at the restaurant and took a seat together at one of the tables. We ordered a bottle of wine to share then looked at the menu.

"What's new with you and that caveman?" Christopher asked as he kept his eyes on the selections.

"Nothing really."

"Are you going to be moving back in with me anytime soon?"

"Why? You want me to?"

He made a disgusted look. "No. I have chicks over all the time. You just cramp my style."

I'd known Christopher long enough to know when he was lying. He hardly did it, so that was how I could figure it out. Christopher and I used to see each other all the time, but after I met Calloway and moved in with him, Christopher and I didn't talk nearly as much as we used to. And we hardly saw each other. "Well, Calloway asked me to move in with him —permanently."

"Really?" He finally set down his menu. "Like, you're staying there indefinitely?"

"Hopefully, forever."

"Oh damn. I guess he's pretty serious, then."

"I think we both are." Sometimes I had my doubts if we could make it work since Calloway preferred me in chains, but I was so head over heels for him that I couldn't think clearly. I'd much rather struggle in a relationship with that man than be with anyone else.

"So, the apartment is totally mine, then?"

"Yep. So you can keep entertaining your lady friends."

"You aren't staying with him just because of Hank?"

When I searched for an apartment to move to, Calloway wasn't pleased with the idea. The situation with Hank didn't seem to have anything to do with our living situation. "No. I don't think Hank will be a problem anymore."

"Did Calloway kill him?" he asked with a straight face.

"Of course not."

"Then you never really know. The guy is a creeper. He'll leave you alone for three months, and then he's in your face again. I wouldn't just assume he's no longer a problem."

"You didn't see how scared he was." I grabbed a

VICTORIA QUINN

piece of bread from the basket and smeared butter across the surface with my knife. "He took one look at Calloway and tucked his tail between his legs. He turned into the biggest pussy I've ever seen."

"For now," Christopher said. "What about when he grows some balls again?"

I took a bite then set the rest of the piece on the plate. "I don't know, Christopher. But I'm not going to live my life in fear all the time. If I do, then he wins."

"I get that, but I don't think we should just assume he's gone either. That's all I'm saying." He snatched the other half of my bread and popped it into his mouth.

"Hey," I said in mock offense.

"You already buttered it and everything. It was just easier."

"But I already took a bite out of it."

He shrugged. "Whatever. I'll take my chances."

We ordered our food then handed the menus over. Once that was taken care of, we talked about work while we drank our wine. Everything was going well until Christopher said something totally out of the blue.

"Okay, fine. I guess I do miss you a little…"

"I knew it." I smiled in triumph.

"I don't really miss living with you," he said. "But we haven't really talked in, like, a month. Gets weird after a while. I'm not saying you don't annoy me, but I guess I kinda need you to annoy me... I know that doesn't make much sense."

"You annoy me too, Christopher. I think siblings need each other in that way."

"Maybe," he said. "And I've been worried about you."

I scoffed because his concern was ridiculous. "Trust me, you don't need to worry about me when Calloway is around."

"But he's not around you every second of the day."

"Actually, he is."

"Is he sitting in your office all day?" he asked incredulously.

"No, but he's down the hall."

"I don't know..." He shook his head. "Hank broke in to our apartment and assaulted you right when everyone got off work. He could have been seen, but he didn't care. I'm sure he was scared of Calloway at the time, but I'm sure he's over it by now."

Maybe he was right, but I chose not to believe it. Calloway would always keep me safe. He was overbearing and obsessive most of the time, but those things came in handy when it came to a stalker ex-boyfriend. Calloway wouldn't let anything slip past his watch. "I think we need to move on with our lives and be more positive."

"Alright, I can take the hint." He looked out the window, consternation etched into his brow. "Other than that, things have been good?"

I didn't mention Calloway's mother because I knew that was private. So I talked about work. "All my colleagues hated me, so Calloway threatened to fire them all if they didn't straighten out."

Christopher chuckled. "Man, I need to start screwing my boss."

"That's the whole reason why they started to hate me. Believe me, they all used to like me at one point."

"I doubt it," he teased.

"I know they're only being nice to me because they have to, but it's still better than the cold shoulder all the time."

"I can imagine. Well, everyone likes me, so I can't totally imagine it, but I get what you mean." He swirled his wine before he took a drink. "Will there be wedding bells and shit in the future?"

"I don't know about that…" For now, we were both living in the moment. We were both trying to make an ordinary relationship work. That was too far into the future for both of us.

"If he asked you to live with him permanently, I'd say he's not opposed to it."

I wasn't really sure. "Sounds like you like him again?"

He shrugged before he drank his wine again. "I thought it was shitty of him to lie to you for so long, but I can tell he really cares about you. He looks after you far better than I ever could. When I see him with you, I can tell he's pussy-whipped. He's done a lot of good to make up for the bad, so yeah, I do like him. Besides, he's rich as fuck."

My body immediately tightened in anger. "That doesn't matter, Christopher."

"Hell yeah, it does. Don't act like a wealthy man is the same as a poor one."

"They are the same. I don't care that Calloway is wealthy."

He rolled his eyes. "All women say that, but they're full of it. Maybe you don't care about the money per se, but the fact that he's ambitious, driven, and smart enough to build his own empire is sexy. Shit, even I think it's sexy. So yes, him being rich does make him more desirable. You're a hard-working woman, Rome. You would be with a man who didn't bust his ass every day just like you have?"

When he put it that way, I saw his point. "I am attracted to his motivation. But not his bank account."

"That's fair. And I know he'll always be able to take care of you."

Christopher meant well, but that statement rubbed me the wrong way. "I will always be able to take care of myself. I've been doing it for a long time."

Christopher masked his reaction by drinking his wine. He looked out the window then abruptly changed the subject, like he was hiding something from me. "I got promoted at work."

The anger immediately disappeared. "Really? Wow, congratulations! Now I have to buy dinner."

"Nah." He brushed it off with a wave of his hand. "I insulted you a lot today. You know, having to get everything out since it'd been so long since I had the opportunity. Besides…" He rubbed his thumb and forefinger together. "I should spend that raise on something good."

"Making me full?" I asked with a smile.

"Yep."

I raised my glass and clinked it against his. "Congratulations, Christopher. You earned it."

"Thanks." He smiled before he took a long drink of his wine. Even though he'd just told me incredible news, he suddenly seemed somber, like something was nagging at him from deep inside.

When I thought about everything that happened

today, I realized Christopher's behavior was out of the ordinary. Now I wondered if there was something bad going on in his life and he was just taking a long time to come clean about it. "What's wrong?" I asked him point-blank because our relationship was strong enough to do that.

He met my look with a guilty one, not surprised that I'd figured it out just from talking with him. "I just —"

The waiter brought our entrees and set them in front of us. He asked us if we needed anything else before he finally walked away.

The moment was just as tense as it had been when the waiter arrived, and I hadn't dropped my look from his face. "Christopher. Honestly, I'm a little worried…"

"It's nothing bad," he said quickly. "I just…I got promoted a few weeks ago, and I realized I had no one to tell."

I didn't have a clue what he meant by that, but I didn't think it was the best time to ask.

"I posted it on social media, but that's not a real person, you know?"

I nodded even though I didn't know what I was agreeing to.

"I wanted to tell you, obviously. But then I remembered you lived with Calloway and you have your own life."

"It doesn't matter if I'm married or have kids. I always want to know what's going on with you, Christopher. You know that."

"Of course I do," he said quickly. "I just meant, outside of you, I don't really have anyone. I don't have a clue who my parents were. I might have sibling somewhere out there. Who knows? But...I don't have a foundation, a family."

A realization slowly dawned upon me. I knew exactly what he was saying because it was something that bothered me my entire life. Christopher was the only thing I had that resembled a family—even if it was based off of poor circumstances.

"Now that you're serious with Calloway, I see how close you guys are. You're more than just two people who are seeing each other. I can tell he loves you just by looking at him. It's obvious you feel the same way."

I knew Calloway loved me even though he refused to say it. It was obvious in every kiss, in every touch. He wouldn't ask me to live with him and spend every waking hour with me if he felt otherwise. And he certainly wouldn't have sacrificed his way of life either. "I understand what you're saying...but I don't see where you're going with this."

"I guess...I guess I want a family."

"A family?"

"Yeah." He nodded. "I guess I want a wife. I never thought I wanted one before, but it would be nice to have someone who loved me, you know? Who wanted to join her life with mine so we could make a family. And then we would have kids...and then I would have someone who actually shares my DNA. I know I sound like a pussy right now—"

"You don't sound anything like a pussy, Christopher." It was incredibly sweet, unbelievably vulnerable. "That's a normal feeling we all have. I want that with Calloway. I want to have a son who looks just like him. I want to be part of someone in a beautiful way. Believe me, I get it."

"It goes against everything I said before..."

"Christopher, men grow out of that phase. Maybe you've grown out of yours."

"I guess..." His glass was empty, so he poured another. "I've never been in a relationship, so I don't know where to start. I've been out with a lot of unbelievable women, but I was an asshole to them, so I blew that."

"There are other fish in the sea."

"Yeah, but even if I found them, I wouldn't know what to do."

"Remember what you said to me?"

He scrunched his eyebrows. "I say a lot of wise

things to you, Rome…"

"You told me a man will change when he meets the right woman." He told me not to worry about Calloway's commitment issues because all of that would disappear once he realized he couldn't live without me. "So, when you meet the right woman, you'll know how to be in a relationship."

"I suppose."

"So don't worry about it. Just don't sleep with them right off the bat."

"You're one to talk," he jabbed.

"Excuse me?" I countered. "Calloway and I waited a long time before we took it to that level."

"Like a day?" he asked incredulously. "That guy is a sexy beast. No way any woman could keep her legs closed."

I was about to express my offense at his comment, but then I realized the more disturbing part of that sentence. "Whoa…did you just check out my boyfriend?"

"No," he said with disgust. "I just know he's a good-looking guy that gets a lot of pussy."

I cringed at the last word of the sentence, disturbed by the idea that Calloway had been with other women before me—a lot of women. "Anyway…Calloway and I waited a month. I didn't want something quick and easy. I fell for him right from the beginning and wanted to make sure it would last."

"A month?" he asked in shock. "I couldn't wait a month with a gun pointed to my head. Maybe a week, but that's still an exaggeration."

"It was just some advice. Take it how you will."

The food finally arrived, and we both ate slowly, saying nothing for a long time. Just sitting with Christopher and being with him was nice. We used to watch TV on the couch together when he didn't have a date for the evening. Silent camaraderie was always the best kind. It was the definition of true compatibility.

"Anything else new with you?" Christopher asked after he finished chewing his food.

"Not really. My life is pretty boring."

"I knew that," he said with a laugh.

I didn't unleash an insult back because I knew I missed it when he teased me. Now that he'd confessed he was lonely in this enormous city, I understood just how much our relationship meant to him. It reminded me that I needed to spend more time with him, to make an effort to remain as close as we'd always been. After everything we'd endured, we couldn't drift apart.

We'd been through too much together.

## 8

CALLOWAY

The moment she was back in the house and in my line of sight, I felt better. Hank probably wouldn't make another appearance because he was a coward. He'd targeted Rome because she was a petite woman, but now that a man like me came with the package, he was powerless to do anything.

I should relax.

But I couldn't do that until she was returned to me in the same condition as when she left.

My arms circled her waist, and I kissed her the second she walked inside, not caring if Christopher looked at us or not. She might be his sister, but she was my woman. I took care of her and adored her, so I could kiss her whenever the fuck I wanted.

When I turned to Christopher, he was staring at a painting on my wall, obviously finding something to look at us besides our affection. "Have a good time?" I shook his hand just as I did when he arrived at the house.

"Eh." He shrugged. "She was a little annoying, but she's been worse." He smiled, telling me he was kidding. "So, I'd say it went pretty well."

"Christopher got promoted at work." Rome stood off to the side, her arms crossed over her chest. She wore a long-sleeve gray sweater that fit snugly over her gorgeous tits. Her brown hair was in spirals as it trailed down her chest, framing her beautiful face. Her green eyes were more vibrant when she did her makeup in a special way. She was gorgeous, and I wasn't sure how Christopher didn't find her attractive. They weren't blood relatives, and they didn't meet until they were teenagers. But it didn't seem like Christopher looked at her in that regard at all.

"Congrats, man." I clapped him on the shoulder. "Good for you."

"Thanks," Christopher answered. "And no, I'm not sleeping with my boss...unlike some people." He shot Rome a look full of accusation.

"I was sleeping with him before he was my boss," Rome countered. "Doesn't count."

"But that's how you got the job, right?" Christopher argued.

I could tell these two were already back to normal. "Want me to call you a cab?"

"Nah." Christopher fist-bumped me before he headed to the door. "I like to walk. More opportunities to spot a beautiful woman." He winked then walked out.

I locked the door behind him as soon as he was gone. When I turned back to Rome, she was standing in the same place, her arms still crossed over her chest. Without even trying, she looked stunning in that sweater and jeans. Something about her natural qualities made her the sexiest woman in the world, with or without clothes. "Have a good time?"

"Yes."

I took a few steps toward her and closed the gap between us. She'd only been gone for a few hours, but that somehow felt like an eternity. I'd worked out in my private gym with music blaring through my headphones, but somehow the distraction wasn't strong enough to make me stop thinking about her.

"What did you do while I was gone?"

"Worked out."

"Ooh…I thought your arms looked nice." Her hand snaked up my arm to my bicep, where she gave the muscle a gentle squeeze.

I wanted to do the same to her tits. "Did he miss you like you assumed?"

"Actually, yes. He told me something interesting…"

I waited for her to answer on her own, refusing to fish for knowledge.

"He said he wants to make his own family. He feels lonely."

"Lonely?" Christopher always struck me as the kind of man who preferred to be alone, like a lone wolf.

"Yeah. Seeing me with you has made him realize I'm not going to be around forever, at least in the way I was before. It's made him feel a little isolated. So now he wants to find a wife and have some kids. You know, start his own family."

I didn't know what to say to that. Christopher didn't strike me as the emotional or sentimental type. But I did have a mother and a brother in my life. I had Ruin, among other things. But when I met Rome, I knew I had to have her, and not because I was lonely. In fact, I never understood I was lonely until she walked through the door. "Didn't realize he was so attached to you."

"I guess I've kinda always known…just never thought about it." She ran her hands up and down her arms slowly, like she was a little chilly.

All she needed was a big, strong man like me to keep

her warm. I moved my arms around her waist and pressed my face close to hers. I didn't like sharing her with anyone—even her brother. My mouth automatically moved to hers, and I kissed her slowly, feeling the heat start deep inside my groin. My tongue danced with hers, and I felt the arousal roll through me like the waves of the ocean during the storm. Images came into my mind, her ass in the air with her hands handcuffed against the small of her back. Her sex glistening with arousal, her pussy anxious for my cock. I paced back and forth at the foot of the bed, my leather belt in my hands. Then I struck her hard on the ass, marking that beautiful skin and turning it a luscious red color.

Fuck.

I pushed the thought from my mind because it was wrong. It was a fantasy, and I shouldn't be thinking about something that wasn't real when I had a woman like Rome right in front of me. She was perfect in every way, enough to satisfy me. I didn't need to picture myself hurting her, listening to her cry and moan at the same time.

No.

"I missed you," she whispered into my mouth.

My hands gripped her tighter than necessary, my desire controlling my behavior. I guided her backward until the backs of her knees hit the couch. I broke our kiss and moved her until her ass hit the cushion.

Like we were of one mind, she reached for my jeans and undid them. My pants and boxers fell to my ankles, and I kicked them away. I was barefoot, so I was ready to go. She gripped my hips then surrounded my cock with her warm mouth, enveloping him in her saliva.

I stared down at her and felt like a king.

She moved her hands to her jeans and undid them, in a hurry to get my cock inside her. Her mouth continued to work over my length at the same time, her experienced tongue still lapping at me without pause.

A new image came to my mind, her hands bound together behind her back with my tie. A blindfold was placed over her face, and she balanced on her knees as she continued to take my cock. I had her hair tight in my palm like she was an animal on a leash.

I shook the thought away.

I yanked her jeans and panties off then moved on top of her on the couch. I placed her legs over my shoulders as I pinned her deep into the cushion, her head against the armrest. When she was curled up underneath me like this, I was insanely turned on. She felt like a prisoner, a plaything.

I brushed my lips over hers before I sank into her, sliding through the slickness that formed the second she walked in the door. With her knees together, she was tighter than usual. My cock was in heaven, feeling her snug slickness.

"Calloway..." She moaned the moment she felt me, her hands gripping my arms for balance.

I loved being buried inside her like this. She was truly mine, my property. I was the first one to fuck her, and I better be the last too. With my eyes trained on her face, I thrust my hips and moved deep inside her, feeling the pussy that I worshiped. I watched every expression she made, every time her lips trembled. If I didn't want to come so badly, I would do this forever. All I could do was last long enough to make her come.

And right on cue, she did.

---

I never mentioned Isabella to Rome, knowing no good would come from it. My view on our physical relationship was perfectly clear, so there was nothing I could say to change Rome's mind about it.

I tried to forget about what Isabella said, but I found it difficult to do.

Like a monster inside me had come to life, the demon couldn't be restrained. I found myself picturing Rome in compromising positions, her ass red and her cheeks stained with tears. I pictured her gaze averted to the floor as she sat on her knees, completely submissive.

It got me so hard I wanted to scream.

I had to fight these urges. I had to fight these dark thoughts. All I had with Rome was vanilla, and I needed to enjoy it, not fantasize about her in shackles.

If I focused hard enough, I could do it.

Right?

My PI called me shortly after lunch, hopefully with news about Hank.

"Hey, Carl. What do you have for me?"

Carl spoke in a bored voice, as was his usual. "It turns out he did have some earlier transgressions with other women. Rome isn't the first."

Of course she wasn't. I didn't need a private investigator to confirm that. "Any evidence?"

"Nothing concrete. Nothing that will work in the court of law, if that's what you mean."

"Would any of these women be willing to come forward?" If they accused him on their own, I wouldn't have to get my hands dirty at all.

"I don't know about that either. I'm sure they're just as afraid of him as Rome was. They would need some encouragement."

Probably a strong man to protect them.

"Anything else?"

"Nope. Rome's past is still a mystery to me. Talked to some contacts but didn't get anywhere."

I hadn't been investigating Rome since she and I turned serious. Anything I wanted to know, she usually told me on her own. It must have slipped my mind to tell Carl to back off. "You don't need to look into her anymore, Carl. But thank you."

"That's a relief," he said. "I can't figure out what her previous name is anyway, so I can't track down any info."

I kept the phone against my ear and paused when I heard what he said. When I first asked him to investigate Rome, he told me her past had been wiped clean after she changed her name. He never figured out why she did it. And the revelation slipped my mind over the course of our relationship.

"Mr. Owens?"

I forgot I was still on the line. "Keep looking into Hank. Don't worry about Rome."

"Alright. Talk to you later."

I hung up without saying goodbye.

Rome told me she had a hard life growing up. That was how she and Christopher crossed paths. But something must be chasing her if she went through all the trouble to wipe away a large portion of her life.

Why hadn't she told me?

I couldn't help but be offended. She waited too long to tell me about Hank, and she was assaulted because of it. Did she have other skeletons in her closet that she was hiding from me? I'd committed my entire life to her. Wasn't that enough to earn her trust?

I wanted to confront her about it, but hesitance immediately took over. The only way I would know this information was if I looked into her background without her permission. I'd known Rome long enough to understand the consequences of that.

She would be livid.

So I would need to fish it out of her some other way. Perhaps if I brought it up over dinner, it would convince her to come clean about whatever she was hiding from. I wasn't trying to be nosy. Of course, I respected her privacy. But if I had another psychopath actively searching for her, I needed to know about it.

I never let anyone catch me with my guard down.

Or I could ask Christopher.

That would be another act of betrayal. Rome wouldn't speak to me for a week if I pulled that stunt. In that case, I may as well just confront her about it directly. Besides, I'd rather hear about it from her anyway.

I finished my workout in the garage and wiped my face with a towel. I stepped into the house, feeling my t-shirt stick to my skin from all the sweat. I patted my face dry then threw the towel over my shoulder. Rome was standing in front of me, wearing black leggings and a pink sports bra. "What's my woman up to?" She looked cute in work-out gear, her hair combed back into a high ponytail. The natural hourglass shape of her figure was sexy. She didn't need to lift a finger, and her body was still unbelievable. I couldn't say the same thing about myself. I needed muscle to be masculine. And muscle didn't just grow on its own.

"Your woman?"

"Yes. That's one of your many names." Sometimes it was sweetheart. Sometimes it was Rome. But when I felt particularly possessive or aroused, it was always woman. It felt more primal to me, carnal, even.

"I was going to hit the gym."

I tried not to smile. "Run on the treadmill?"

"Hey, I can lift weights too. I'm not totally clueless."

"Just be careful. A lot of that stuff is heavy."

She rolled her eyes and walked past me, shaking her hips as she went.

I smacked her ass as she moved by me, feeling that tight ass. "I'm gonna shower. You know where to find me."

"I'm gonna get hot and sweaty. You know where to find me."

I walked into my bedroom then got in the shower. The second the warm water hit me, I pictured Rome getting a very different workout. She didn't need a gym or free weights. If we went to my playroom at Ruin, she would get all the cardio she needed.

My cock was hard the second I touched her ass, and now it was even harder because my thoughts turned sinister. I wanted to shove a butt plug up her ass and stare at the shiny jewel while I fucked her cunt. Feeling full at both ends would make her come so hard, she would scream and lose her voice.

My cock twitched.

I massaged the shampoo into my hair and forced myself not to think such dirty things. My cock was rock hard and swollen at the head. I hadn't wanted to jerk off since I met Rome, but now the need possessed me. I wanted to live out my fantasy, even if it wasn't real.

I couldn't.

Like my cock had dominion over my brain, I pictured her riding me then slapping me as hard as she could. She slapped me harder than she ever did in that bar. Her handprint was permanently etched into my cheek.

I tilted my head under the water and felt the soap

drift down my body. My hands shook because I couldn't fight the temptation. I knew Rome was in the garage and would remain there for at least thirty minutes.

I had time to rub one out.

I felt like an asshole for having the urge, for pleasuring myself when I had the perfect woman to satisfy me. But fuck, I wanted to do kinky shit that she wouldn't allow. With a clenched jaw and a guilty conscience, I squirted the shampoo into my hand and lathered it onto my dick.

Now that I allowed my mind to think these debauched things, the images came immediately. I gripped my belt and smacked it hard against her ass, hearing her whimper with tears. *Count with me.*

*One.*

I gripped the belt again then slapped it across her other cheek, making a mark where I struck her. *Louder.*

*Two…*

I hit her again and again, punishing her for not telling me about her past. I was her Dom, and she was supposed to tell me every little detail about her life. She was supposed to seek me out for protection, to confide every secret to me. I hit harder than ever before, my knuckles turning white because I gripped the leather so hard.

She released a cry and a moan at the exact same time. *Three.*

I dropped the belt then came up behind her at the foot of the bed. I shoved my raging cock inside her and felt the slickness immediately. She was soaked and desperate for my length. She knew she deserved to be punished. She knew she deserved three more slaps once I was finished fucking her.

My hand moved up and down my length quickly, matching the pace that I fucked her in my mind. Her pussy was so tight and wet. Hear screams echoed in my head. I stuck two fingers in my mouth and sucked before I shoved them deep inside her tight little asshole. That made her moan again, and my cock was about to explode.

I was right on the edge of an explosion. I could feel the desire pool in my balls before it shot down my length. My entire body felt amazing, felt incredible. I came so hard I couldn't stop myself from releasing a moan. I shot onto the shower wall, the white come sticking to the tile before it slowly slipped down to the drain. I kept rubbing myself until every drop was gone, picturing her tight pussy taking the entire load. "Fuck..." I leaned against the wall when I was finished, relieved and satisfied. Now that I'd finally gotten what I needed maybe I would stop thinking those dirty thoughts.

Or maybe they would just get worse.

---

"I'm so sore, I can barely move." Rome lay beside me in bed, on her side with her back to me. She reminded me of a pregnant woman who was uncomfortable during the end of her pregnancy.

"I told you those weights were heavy."

"I'll stick to the treadmill next time."

I pressed my chest against her back and cuddled her in the dark. I made love to her after dinner, right on the dining table where our plates had been moments before. We'd probably have another round now if she wasn't so stiff. If I hadn't treated myself that afternoon, I'd probably be much grouchier.

Even when we lay together like this in peaceful union, I couldn't help but wonder what her real name was. Was Rome even her first name? Had it been something else entirely? Did Christopher call her something else when they were alone together?

The fact that he knew something that I didn't know bothered me.

I lay with my face pressed into her hair, her scent

washing over me in comforting waves. When she was beside me, I slept so much better. I descended into the land of a dreamless sleep. Even when she turned in the middle of the night and smacked my cheek with her palm, I still loved the closeness. When she was really tired, she snored. I loved that too.

Even though Rome wasn't looking at me, she could feel my tension. It filled the dark room and infected her skin. "Something on your mind?"

I didn't know how to address this topic. It could easily push her away, and I would end up sleeping alone for the night. "You and Christopher were in the same foster home, right?"

She flinched at the question, like that was the last thing she expected me to say. "Why do you ask?"

"It's an important aspect of your life. I want to know everything about you."

"Well, I already told you we were in the same foster home. Then we were adopted together later on."

It was obvious she didn't want to talk about this. Her tone was short and clipped. She was pushing me away, closing me off. I didn't appreciate it. "You can tell me anything. I hope you know that, Rome."

"I know, Calloway. But there's nothing to tell. That part of my life is over."

Was anything ever really over? I hid my offense that

she continued to keep her secret from me. If she thought I wouldn't figure it out eventually, she wasn't very bright. The truth always found its way to the surface—every time. I struggled to keep my anger at bay at the cold brush-off. I'd made a lot of sacrifices for this relationship, but that still wasn't good enough for her.

I didn't say another word for the rest of the evening.

## 9

ROME

Calloway walked inside my office on Friday after five. He did his usual routine by standing in silence near the doorway and letting his brooding exterior do all the talking. He'd been in a sour mood all week. Every time I asked him about it, he claimed he was just tired.

I grabbed my things and met him at the door. "Thank god it's Friday, huh?"

He stared down at my face, his eyes narrowed on my lips. He leaned in and kissed me, the kind that was longer and harder than it should be for the office. Then he abruptly pulled away without responding to my comment. "We need to pick up a dress for you." He walked into the hallway and slowed his pace so I could keep up with him.

"A dress?"

"We have charity gala tomorrow night."

I'd completely forgotten about it. "Oh yeah…"

We entered the elevator and rode it to the lobby. "There's a few boutiques down the street. I'm sure we'll find something for you."

"I can go on my own, Calloway. No reason to bore you."

"Watching my woman try on beautiful gowns isn't boring for me." We left the building then walked up the street together, merging with the rest of the pedestrians as they left work to enjoy their weekend.

"What a diplomatic answer."

He circled his arm around my waist, his large hand heavy against my hip. "I've never been much of a diplomat."

We walked into one of the high-end shops in Manhattan. I could tell just by looking at the mannequins that I couldn't even afford a scarf. Designer logos were on the wall, the kind of quality that celebrities wore on the red carpet. "Calloway, I —"

"My treat. Don't worry about it." He read my mind like he was sitting inside my brain at that very moment.

"It's a charity event. Don't you think it's insensitive to wear a designer gown?"

"Not at all. It's being held at the Plaza, remember?"

He walked up to the front counter and immediately got the attention of the woman standing behind it. "My girlfriend needs a gown for tomorrow evening. She's a size two."

I raised an eyebrow. "How do you know what size I am?"

He pressed his lips to my ear. "I fuck you every night, don't I?"

"Of course, sir." The saleswoman came around the counter in a pencil skirt and black-framed glasses. It wasn't the kind of service I was used to getting at the local mall. "What's the occasion?"

"Charity gala," Calloway said. "Price isn't an object. I want something elegant but a little revealing." He winked before he pressed a kiss to my shoulder. "I'll be in the waiting area. Let me know when you're ready." He walked away, looking like he owned the store the second he walked inside it. His shoulders seemed more powerful every single time I looked at them.

I turned back to the woman who was in charge of dressing me up. The sizzle of attraction was in her eyes, not immune to Calloway's charms like she should be. When she caught my look, she quickly pretended like her eyes weren't just glued to his tight ass. "This way. I already have something in mind…"

I never looked at the price tag because I would throw up if I did. I felt guilty for letting him buy me something I didn't even need. But it seemed important to him that I look my best. And deep down inside, I was excited to own something so glamorous. I'd always been a bargain shopper because I was satisfied knowing I wouldn't have the nicer things in my life. But the moment I got to get my hands on something truly beautiful, I felt the flutter in my chest.

Calloway handed over his credit card without blinking then carried the gown out of the store. "You're gonna look perfect in this tomorrow tonight." He stopped at the edge of the sidewalk then pulled out his phone. He typed a quick message, probably to Tom, before he shoved it back inside his pocket.

"Thanks...I really love it. Thank you for getting it for me." He already did so much for me. There was no way I could ever repay him for his kindness. He gave me a job when he didn't have to. He let me live with him and wouldn't accept any money for my half of his mortgage. He paid for all our groceries and our meals. It was strange to have a savings account when I'd barely had enough to get by most weeks for most of my life.

His arm circled my waist, and he pressed a warm kiss to my temple. His lips were seductive, exquisite to the touch. "It was my pleasure, sweetheart. I just hope no man makes the mistake of staring at you too long. The charity gala will turn into a crime scene."

"Well, that woman in there was staring at your ass, so I'd say we're even."

Calloway looked up the street as he waited for his driver, neither confirming nor denying that he knew the saleswoman had the hots for him. It was a smart move.

"We can just walk," I said. "I don't mind." My heels hurt my feet, but I'd been walking the streets of Manhattan for so long that I was used to it.

"You aren't walking in those. I'm not sure how you get through the day at the office."

"Well...I sit most of the time."

"Wish you were sitting on my face." He looked down at me, the corner of his mouth raised in the form of a smile.

I knew he was only partially joking. "Neither one of us would get anything done."

The car pulled up, and Calloway opened the back door for me. "I was never a good worker anyway." He got in the seat beside me then moved his hand to my thigh. My gown was hooked to the hanger inside the car so it wouldn't get wrinkled. He couldn't look out the window because the dress was in the way, so he chose to stare at me instead.

I couldn't ignore his look because it was so powerful. When he commanded my attention, he always got it. Even if I wasn't looking directly at him, I was still giving him my full attention. When the stare became too much, I met his gaze.

He circled his arm around my shoulders and moved his other hand to my thigh. He slowly inched his hand up my leg, moving underneath the material as he pressed his face to mine. When his lips were just inches from mine, he teased me with their proximity. His hand slowly slid farther up until his fingers touched the outside of my panties.

The center divider was up so the driver couldn't see what we were doing in the back, but I still felt naughty anyway. If Calloway made me scream loud enough, Tom was certain to hear it.

He still didn't kiss me, just brushing his lips past mine as his fingers touched me. His thumb pulled my panties to the side, and his fingertips finally touched my throbbing sex.

I moaned into his face and felt my knees widen automatically. My hand gripped his bicep just so I had something to latch on to.

His fingers rubbed my clit as he brushed his mouth against mine.

I loved the feeling of his fingers but I wanted his mouth just as much. My arm circled his neck, and I pulled his lips against mine, finally getting the kiss I was anxious to have. I should feel on display since this was one of the most public places we'd ever fooled around, but when Calloway's hands were on me, I couldn't think clearly.

He rubbed me harder, bringing me to the edge of a sweet climax.

Then he abruptly pulled away, taking his lips and fingers. He sat beside me and faced forward again, like nothing had just happened.

"Uh...excuse me?" He'd never left me hanging before, so I couldn't hide the shock.

His face remained hard, unyielding. "Think about that way on the rest of the ride home. I'll fuck you when we get there."

"What kind of game is this?"

"No game, sweetheart."

I pressed my knees together and squeezed my thighs, feeling my sex throb with angry desire. I seriously considered finishing the job myself, but I knew it would feel so much better if I let Calloway have the honors. "Why are you doing this to me? I thought you were a gentleman?"

"Trust me, the wait will be worth it."

"I don't agree..."

He turned back to me, his face so handsome it hurt to look at him. "The second we walk through that door, I'll fuck you up against that wall. I'm gonna come as soon as I'm inside you—and you're gonna come too."

---

I did my hair and makeup in the other bathroom since Calloway was getting ready at the same time. I'd never attended one of these fancy events, the kind with flutes of champagne and men in tuxedos. Since I was from humble beginnings, this was all new to me. I spent extra time making my hair perfect, and I wore more makeup than I normally would. I just hoped I didn't overdo it.

The dress Calloway bought me was sleeveless with a sweetheart top. It was tight around my waist then flared out once it reached my hips. It was a soft gold color with black highlights, stunning but subtle at the same time.

I never wanted to take it off.

I walked downstairs and slipped on my heels, feeling five inches taller the second they were on. I was organizing my clutch when I heard Calloway reach the bottom stair behind me. "I'm ready whenever you are."

He came up behind me and pressed his lips against the back of my neck. His hand moved to my hips where he gripped me tightly, digging his fingers right through the fabric and into my skin. He held me like that for nearly a minute, just breathing with me. "I haven't even seen your face, and you still look beautiful."

"I hope you don't prefer me that way," I teased.

He chuckled against my neck. "I do sometimes—but not right now." He guided my hips with his hands and turned me around until I faced him. The arrogant smile that was on his face slowly faded away, replaced with a softer expression I rarely saw. His hand moved to my neck where he gently laid his fingers against my warm skin, his thumb right over my pulse. He didn't make a comment because it wasn't necessary. His thoughts were written on his face like text on a page.

My hand moved around his wrist so I could feel his pulse, noticing how soft and rhythmic it was. When I gripped him during lovemaking, it was usually pounding with adrenaline. Now I could feel a gentle side of him.

"I don't think I can wait until the end of the night to make love to you, sweetheart." He came closer to me until his face was pressed to mine. He didn't kiss me, but his lips were close enough that I could feel the magnetic pull between our mouths.

I didn't know how much time we had, but I realized I didn't really care. I'd spent an hour doing my hair and makeup, but now I didn't care about messing it up. When he looked at me like that, all I wanted was to be united with him. "Then don't."

## 10

# CALLOWAY

I did my best to keep her dress nice and not mess up her hair, which she spent nearly an hour doing. I took her at the foot of the bed with my slacks around my ankles and my collared shirt wide open. My jacket had been laid on the bed instead of tossed on the floor where I would normally throw it.

I wasn't in the mood to fuck her, not like I usually was. When I saw how beautiful she looked, so elegant and exquisite, my heart did a strange somersault. I just wanted to be buried inside her, to feel my woman in a way no one else ever had.

I moved my enormous length deep inside her slowly, nearly hitting her in the cervix before I pulled out again. Her arousal was drenched around me, and she was tight like she always was. In the moment, I didn't care about the charity gala. If I walked in late, I didn't give a shit. When I wanted my woman, I took her. There was no way in hell I was going to wait until the end of the evening. Knowing me, we would just hook up in the bathroom anyway.

And her dress would definitely get dirty then.

She lay absolutely still so she wouldn't mess up her hair, but when she started to climax, she arched her body and tilted her head, her expression utterly sexy. "Calloway…"

Fuck, I loved it when she said my name.

I enjoyed the rest of the show, watching her writhe and ride the high until she was completely finished.

I finally forgot I was pissed at her for not telling me the truth about her past, for not telling me her real name. When we were connected like this, man and woman, her secrets seemed irrelevant. My obsession rekindled to new heights, and I enjoyed her just the way I used to.

I would have kept going if we didn't have anywhere to be. But since we did, I knew it was time to finish. I continued my slow pumps until my cock thickened and it was hard as steel. It was the best part about the orgasm, about the exquisite explosion in my cock before I finally released.

I hit my threshold then released inside her, filling her with all of my come, where it would remain for the rest of the night. I would show her off to my respected colleagues and donors, knowing she was full of my seed. It would make me feel like a man.

My woman always made me feel like a man.

---

She sat beside me in the middle seat of the car as my driver drove us to the Plaza. My hand rested on her thigh, and I glanced down at her from time to time, wondering what she was thinking in that pretty little head of hers. She looked like a beauty queen beside me, making me appear unremarkable in comparison.

We pulled up to the front of the hotel where a few guests were chatting. Men in suits with women in gowns on their arms. One of the attendants opened the door so I could step up. Before he could help Rome out of the car, I extended my hand and helped her emerge like the royalty that she was.

The attendant looked at her with approval before he walked to the next car that just pulled up.

My arm circled her waist, and I held her close into my side, wanting it to be completely obvious that she was more than just my date—she was the woman who slept in my bed every night. We moved through the entrance then headed to the grand ballroom where the dinner was being held.

"So, is this a silent auction or something?"

"No." I noticed the way her hair would brush against my arm. I couldn't feel it through my suit, but I knew how it felt because it happened when we slept together every night. Her soft strands prickled my skin with their innate softness. "It's to recognize the outstanding donors for the last year. Usually, other people who come forward and make big donations so their company can have that same publicity at a later time. The whole thing is a PR stunt, honestly."

"I'm sure some people genuinely want to give back."

Some, but not most. "Or get a tax break."

"Oh, come on." She bumped her hip into my side. "Give humanity more credit than that."

"I already was."

She rolled her eyes like I was joking.

I was being dead serious.

We entered the ballroom where hundreds of people chitchatted with colleagues or introduced themselves to corporate competitors. I recognized some of the people from my company mingling with the people who gave us the donations to make our work possible. Crystal chandeliers hung from the ceiling, and the tables were covered with ivory tablecloths and beautiful flowers as centerpieces.

But I cared more about the bar.

I guided my date to where the liquor was held. "What would you like, sweetheart?"

"Whatever you're having." The way she smiled when she spoke made me want to kiss her—and kiss her hard.

But I would do that later. I got the drinks then handed one to her.

She looked at me as she sipped from her glass, a coy expression in her eyes.

I could tell she was flirting with me without saying a single word. She did that when we were in public places sometimes. If she thought I wouldn't fuck her in the bathroom because we made love before we left the house, she was dead wrong.

Before I could express my threat, people recognized me and moved my way for a conversation.

But there was still the rest of the night.

---

"You know a lot of people." Rome and I finally got a moment to ourselves when I excused us to get another drink.

"I don't. But they know me."

"Then how do you remember them all?"

"I write it down on my hand." I gave her a teasing look before I handed her another glass.

She rolled her eyes then sipped her drink. "How much money do you think we'll raise tonight?"

That was always her end game. She wanted to know what kind of difference we were going to make for the people who needed the most help. Fancy dinners with people dressed in their finest wasn't interesting to her. It was one of her attributes that made me fall for her a long time ago. "A lot."

"Does that go directly to us?"

"Not necessarily. Some of it will go directly to certain groups, like the American Red Cross, Salvation Army, etc."

"Oh, okay."

"The money will be allocated appropriately." My arm hardly left her waist all night, wanting to show her off to everyone in the room. I'd never taken a date to these sorts of things. It was much easier to come alone and mingle. But now I never went anywhere without my better half.

We walked to one of the tables, and I pulled out the chair for her. Just as she sat down, I noticed a familiar face across the room. With dark hair, blue eyes, and a strong frame, he blended in with the rest of the suits in the crowd. But his terrified expression made him stand out to me.

Hank.

He was the last person I expected to see here. Maybe he came to these events regularly, but I never noticed because he didn't mean anything to me at the time. But he must have known I would be here—thinking he was safe with all these witnesses.

Think again, motherfucker.

Rome noticed my gaze and emitted a quiet gasp when she realized who was on the receiving end. "Calloway, don't—"

I already left the table. I slowly walked around groups of people and other tables as I made my way toward him.

His eyes nearly popped out of his head, and he turned around and darted the other way.

Pussy shit.

I walked at a normal pace and smiled when I saw colleagues do the same to me. But I never took my eyes off my target. I watched him move through people until he reached the mayor. He stood beside him and struck up a random conversation, his drink still in hand. He'd spilled a few drops on his suit during his attempt to flee.

Like the goddamn mayor would stop me. He could

be the president of the United States, and I still wouldn't give a shit.

I walked up to the group, right beside Hank, and stared him down.

Michael Rosenberg turned to me once I joined the group. "Mr. Owens, how are you this fine evening?" The mayor stuck out his hand to shake mine.

I took it with a firm grip. "I'm wonderful, sir. How are you?"

"Great. I'm always in a good mood when there's an open bar."

Hank continued to stand there, sweat forming on his forehead.

I stared him down, enjoying every single second of his terror. That was exactly how Rome felt when she looked over her shoulder every day. I wanted him to suffer worse than she ever had. He needed broken bones and hideous scars. "How's Lydia?"

Michael didn't seem to care that I was staring at Hank instead of him. "She's good. She's mingling with the girls. You know how women get. I probably won't see her until the end of the night."

"I do," I said in agreement.

"You brought someone?" the mayor asked. "That's wonderful, Calloway. May I meet her?"

I turned back to Michael, so grateful he asked that

question. "Of course." I turned to where Rome sat at the table, her eyes trained on my conversation with alarm in her eyes. I held up my hand and beckoned her with my fingers.

Rome's eyes doubled in size.

I gave her a hard look, telling she better get her ass over here or I'd drag her.

She eventually rose out of the chair and walked around the edge of the tables toward us.

I eyed Hank, seeing his clammy skin and the anxiety in his eyes.

Rome finally came to my side, stiff and obviously terrified of the man who stood right beside me. She wore a fake smile, but her eyes were filled with dread.

My arm immediately circled her waist, and I pulled her into my side, reminding her nothing could happen to her when she was in my possession. "Michael, this is Rome. Rome, this is Michael Rosenberg, the major of New York."

Rome did her best to be herself, but she came off as nervous. "It's a pleasure to meet you, sir." She shook his hand before she squeezed back into my side. "You've done a lot for the people of New York, and I appreciate it."

"Thank you," Michael said. "Calloway, she's lovely."

"Thank you, sir." I eyed Hank again, challenging

him with just my silence. He thought he was safe when he was next to powerful men of this city. But he didn't realize I knew these same people—and I was more powerful than all of them.

I suspected Rome had never been this close to Hank unless they were in the middle of a brawl. She did her best to appear calm, but I could feel the slight tremor in her frame. The woman I knew wasn't afraid of anything, and if she was afraid, she didn't show it. So this reaction just made me want to break Hank's neck even more. No woman should ever have to feel like prey like this.

"Well, I need to talk with a few friends," Michael said. "But maybe we can hit the links together next week."

"I'd love to, sir." I shook his hand again. "I'll have my assistant call your assistant."

"Sounds good." Michael turned around, his back to us.

Hank had been silent for the entire conversation. I thought it was odd that the mayor didn't find that abnormal. Hank immediately darted away so he could get away from us.

I snatched him by the arm and yanked him back, forcing more of his wine to hit the front of his suit. I didn't give a damn if anyone saw what I did. It happened so quickly that people probably weren't sure what they saw.

Rome held her breath beside me, petrified of what would happen next.

I looked Hank in the eye, doing my best not to crush my massive fist against his face. "You picked the wrong woman to fuck with, Hank."

---

We finished dinner as the speeches began. Awards were given out, and outstanding contributors to society were recognized. The ceremony seemed to stretch on interminably with no end in sight.

I kept my hand on Rome's thigh, reminding her I was always there. I was an invisible concrete wall around her, so thick and powerful that nothing could break through. She would always be safe under my protection.

Rome did her best to behave normally, but she didn't smile again for the rest of the night. She didn't say a word to me either, eating in silence and never meeting my gaze. She probably wanted to leave so she wouldn't have sit in the same room as that horrible human being.

But we couldn't leave.

VICTORIA QUINN

There wasn't a statement more powerful than holding our ground. I'd proven that I wasn't afraid of him, that a ballroom full of witnesses didn't change my treatment of him. And Rome proved that she wouldn't run either.

We just had to get through the rest of the night.

I pressed my face to her temple and kissed her hairline, comforting her in the only way I knew how at the moment.

My touch didn't make her melt like it usually did. Like she was frozen, she didn't feel anything. "I need to use the restroom." She tossed her napkin on the table and excused herself.

Of course, I followed her.

Our table was near the edge, so leaving the ballroom without distracting anyone else was easy. I trailed behind her and watched her hips shake as she walked in her sky-high heels. When we exited the room, I caught up to her and moved my arm around her waist.

She darted out of my hold and into the bathroom, like my touch was the last thing she wanted.

I felt the offense burn into my skin at her rejection. She didn't need anything else but me to get through this. I put my hands in my pockets as I waited for her, wondering if she was crying inside the women's restroom.

I only lasted a few minutes before I walked inside and joined her.

She stood at the sink with her hands resting against the counter. Her head was tilted to the sink, and she breathed slowly. There were no tears, but she obviously needed the privacy of the bathroom to get a hold of the emotions she was battling deep inside.

I glanced underneath the stalls and realized we were alone. I kept my distance and crossed my arms over my chest, standing at the opposite end of the counter so she would still have space if she needed it.

She finally noticed my approach and turned to me. "Sorry…I just wanted a moment where I didn't have to put on a face."

"I understand." Wearing a mask took energy. Pretending to feel one emotion when you felt the complete opposite was exhausting. I did it from time to time. "But we can't leave, Rome. We need to back in there and stay for the rest of the evening."

"I know…"

"There's absolutely no reason to be scared." As long as I was alive, I would make sure he never bothered her again. There wasn't anything he could do to get through me. Even a bullet wouldn't stop me.

"I know that too."

"That guy is a goddamn pussy. He's not gonna

bother you anymore." Hank didn't put up a fight whatsoever. He only harassed Rome because she was smaller than he was. But when he came face-to-face with a real opponent, he ran for the hills. It was absolutely pathetic. "He knows I have just as much as power. He knows I know the same people. If he makes another move, and I catch him in the act, he'll be done for. He knows it. I know it."

She finally turned back to me, looking breathtaking even when she was worked up. The dress was tight around her petite waist, and her hair was still luscious and thick. I wanted to kiss away all her fears. "I wouldn't know what to do without you, Calloway..."

My eyes softened.

"I've never needed a man for anything." She looked at the ground because she couldn't look at me anymore. "But...I need you for everything."

The vulnerability in her voice went straight to my heart. She hardly ever admitted weakness to anyone, even me. But she confessed her soul to me, told me her truest and darkest feelings. My heart did a strange thing in that moment. It tightened and ached like she hurt me rather than flattered me. Knowing this fiercely independent and powerful woman needed me filled me with a strange sense of joy. Once I laid eyes on her, I wanted to be everything that she was missing. I wanted to fix everything that was broken. I wanted to give her a life she deserved.

And I knew why.

I joined her where she stood in front of the sink and cupped her face. Instead of kissing her, I pressed my forehead to hers and closed my eyes, savoring the powerful connection between us. Without feeling her pulse, I could feel her heartbeat. Without feeling her soul, I could feel her love. This woman was the most beautiful thing I possessed, the rarest diamond in a sea of jewels. I loved to worship her and protect her, and knowing she wanted me to do those things gave me a sense of fulfillment.

The words sat on the edge of my tongue, but I couldn't say them. I felt the sensation deep inside my soul, the raw feeling of devotion. The emotion rushed through my entire body, but my mouth still wouldn't react. The feeling was so foreign and so powerful I didn't know how to assuage my fear.

So I didn't say it.

But I certainly felt it.

"I love you too, Calloway."

I opened my eyes and looked at her, seeing the love written on her gorgeous features. Her emerald eyes lit up like gems. They reflected the fluorescent lights from the ceiling, so they were even brighter than usual. She looked so strong and so vulnerable at the same time.

Words left me in that moment, so I did the only thing I could do. I kissed her on the forehead and rested my lips there, continuing to stand in the public restroom with her. If someone walked in, I couldn't care less.

And neither could she.

At the end of the evening, we left the ballroom and entered the main lobby of the hotel. Rome's hand was in my grasp as she walked in her heels. Even with the extra five inches added to her height, she was still nearly a foot shorter than me.

"I can't wait to go home," she whispered near my ear.

"Yeah?"

"These shoes are gorgeous, but they're killing me."

"I could always carry you."

"No, I'll manage."

We walked outside, and I texted my driver to come get us.

Hank walked out with another attorney from the office, a guy I recognized but couldn't recall by name.

When he noticed us nearby, he purposely veered off to the left to avoid being close to Rome and me.

I stared him down the entire time.

It was safe to say Hank wouldn't be a problem anymore. He used to torture Rome because it was easy, but now that I was around, his taunts were no longer effective. He didn't want to go head-to-head with me because he would lose.

But I still wanted retribution.

I wanted him to pay for what he'd done to Rome. He knocked her around and put her in the hospital for two days. We both needed justice for that. I wanted to unleash my vengeance physically, but I understood the risk of doing that. As one of the best lawyers in the city, he could easily use the justice system to his advantage. If things didn't go well for me, I could be locked up for a short amount of time. And if that did happen, Rome would be completely vulnerable on her own.

So violence wasn't an option for me.

I would have to learn to let my rage go. The important thing was, he was finally leaving her alone. If he made a false move, I would document every little thing he did and take it to court. So we were both waiting for the other to make a mistake and incriminate himself first. I suspected we were both too smart for such stupidity.

The car arrived, and I opened the back door for Rome, allowing her to get in first. I gave Hank a final threatening look before I joined her in the back seat. Even once I was in the car, I continued to stare him down. The windows were tinted so he couldn't see me, but I was certain he could feel the target trained right on his chest.

The car pulled away, and we headed home.

Rome slipped off her heels then massaged her feet. "If I had to wear those any longer, I would have chopped off my feet."

I grabbed her by the ankle and moved her feet to my lap. Just in case my driver saw more than he should, I hit the button and rolled up the divider between us so we would have privacy. My hands worked the soles of her feet and the arch in her foot.

"You don't need to do that..." She lay back and immediately closed her eyes, her words meaningless.

"I like touching you."

"Mmm..." She rested her head on her folded arms and didn't say anything else during the drive home.

I continued to use my thumbs to massage her petite feet, loving the way they felt in my hands. I was never a feet kind of guy, but when it came to Rome, I loved everything. From her fingers to her toes, she was perfect.

We arrived at the house moments later, and Rome had to force herself to sit up. "You can do incredible things with your hands, Calloway."

I chuckled then got out. "I've heard that before." I grabbed her hand and helped her out. She carried her heels in one hand and stepped on the sidewalk barefoot. I scooped her up effortlessly then walked to the front door. She was light enough that I got the door unlocked with one hand and carried her over the threshold.

"Thanks for the lift."

Instead of putting her down in the entryway, I carried her upstairs and to the bedroom she now shared with me. I set her on the ground then immediately unzipped her dress. As much as I loved seeing it on her, I wanted her naked for me to enjoy.

The dress fell into a pile on the floor, and I kissed her bare shoulder, her skin warm to the touch. I felt her body tighten in response, the excitement running through her veins. Her breathing changed instantly, the spark filling the air.

It was one of the rare times when I sincerely wanted to make love, to have slow and sensual sex that was plain vanilla. I didn't picture her chained to the headboard with a blindfold over her eyes. I didn't imagine her suspended from the ceiling with her feet hanging inches off the ground. I didn't have to pretend to hurt her to get off. I wanted it like this, when it was just her and me in the moment.

Hopefully, my struggle had passed. I jerked off in the shower a few weeks ago because I couldn't control the urge that I had. I needed to fulfill the fantasy, to at least pretend I was getting what I needed. I felt ashamed for what I did afterward, but when I knew she was keeping a secret from me, that guilt faded.

Now I didn't think about it.

After we were both undressed, I got her on her back on the bed, her head resting on the pillow. Her legs were spread, and I positioned myself right at her entrance. I wanted to be inside her all night long, to fill her with everything I had until there was nothing left.

Anxious, she gripped my hips and pulled me inside her, forcing my cock past her lips and through her slickness. She bit her bottom lip as she felt my thick cock fill her narrow channel. Her breathing picked up quickly, a quiet pant filling the bedroom.

I savored the sensation even though I'd felt it a hundred times. Before we left for the dinner, I'd made love to her on this same bed. That was just a few hours ago, but now I was hungry like it had never happened at all.

Rome grabbed her tits and played with them for me to watch. She made the sexiest expressions during sex.

Her eyes became lidded and heavy with pleasure, and her lips parted with every moan she made.

I moved my arms behind her knees and pinned her thighs back so I could give her more of my cock. It didn't matter how tight and narrow she was. I was going to give her every inch because she was my woman.

Her hands loosened from her tits as the momentum swept over her. It was obvious to me when she was going to come. Not only did her pussy constrict around my cock like a snake around its prey, but her body arched and her head rolled back. Her lips slightly parted from the deep breath she took. Right when the force hit her, she screamed.

"Calloway..." Her hands moved to my arms, and she dug her nails into my wrists as she rode the high. "Calloway."

There was nothing sexier than listening to her call out my name. "Sweetheart...I love making love to you." I silenced her screams with my kiss, my tongue darting into her mouth as I continued to ram my cock inside her.

Her nails continued to dig into me until she finally rode out the explosion that happened between her legs. She caught her breath and slowly wound down, her pussy flooded with moisture that her body released.

I had wanted to keep going, but now I just wanted to come. Knowing me, I would be hard again in a few moments anyway. When I had a woman like this underneath me, it didn't take much to get me hard even if I'd just come minutes ago. "Fuck, I want to come."

"Allow me to help." She rolled me to my back then crawled on top of me.

I liked being on top and watching her tits shake underneath me, but I loved the view when I was on the bottom. She knew how to ride cock like a pro. If I didn't know she was a virgin before she met me, I never would have suspected it.

Her knees straddled my hips, and she pointed my cock at her entrance. She slowly slid down like she was inserting him for the first time. My cock was soaked in her slickness so it slid right in again.

She rolled her hips as she took my length over and over. Her hands moved to her tits, and she played with them, her thumbs sliding across her nipples and making them pebble. Her hair was beautiful around her shoulders, and her expression was undeniably erotic. She took my length all the way to my balls then raised her body to reach my head. Then she lowered herself again.

I gripped her ass and guided her down my length at the speed I liked. I was eager to come, and I wanted it fast. I moved her body until her tits shook like crazy. I moaned and panted with her, my cock hardening to such a degree it actually hurt. "Here it comes…"

She reached her hand behind her and stroked my balls as she continued to sit on my length. "I'm ready."

I gripped her hips as I released, filling her pussy with all the come I'd been storing for the night. I dumped all of it inside her, moaning uncontrollably as if I hadn't gotten laid in months. There was something about her pussy that made me addicted to a frightening degree. "Fuck…" I pulled her hips down harder so she wouldn't miss a single drop.

She leaned over me with my cock still inside her and pressed a kiss to my lips. "You're an amazing man." She pressed kisses along my jaw and down my neck, moving to my chest and shoulders. Her soft lips sprinkled her affection everywhere, making my ego inflate as this gorgeous woman worshiped me like I'd done something to deserve it.

"You're the one who makes me amazing."

## 11

ROME

We'd visited Theresa nearly every day for the past three weeks. Sometimes we skipped the visit because we were both tired or busy. Unfortunately, it didn't seem like it mattered how many times we visited her.

She still didn't remember us.

We checked in with her nurse then met her on the back patio. Now that I'd spent so much time with her, I realized I'd never seen her in any other location. She was never inside her apartment, always outside—rain or shine.

Calloway introduced himself with a smile even though he'd done it at least a thousand times now.

Now that I'd made the same introductions, listened to the same Harry Potter book, and listened to her ask the same questions every single time, I understood why this was so difficult for Calloway. Not only was it repetitive, but it was meaningless. His relationship with his mother never grew. It was permanently stuck in the same routine.

Calloway read the first chapter as Theresa and I listened. I'd heard this story so many times that I concentrated on Calloway's voice and the way his mouth moved instead. I noticed the way he held the paperback with ease, the veins in his hands powerful and noticeable. I paid attention to the man I'd fallen so madly in love with, oblivious to everything else in the world. He was the first man who was worth my trust, worth my loyalty. Now I hardly had any more walls around my heart.

Theresa stared over the edge of the balcony and to the garden of flowers below. She played with a pendant on her necklace, gliding it back and forth so she had something to do with her hands. I noticed the traits she shared with Calloway—the blue eyes, the natural intensity, and the innate intelligence. I couldn't thank her enough for making a man like him.

Calloway kept reading until Theresa slowly closed her eyes and leaned her head against the back of the rocking chair. Her fingers stopped playing with the necklace as her hand relaxed. Her breathing was deep and even, showing that she drifted off to a peaceful place.

Calloway stopped reading once he noticed he'd put his mother to sleep. He rested the book on his knee and watched her with a soft expression he never showed for anyone else. As cold and hard as Calloway was, he definitely had a soft spot for his mother.

I thought it was sweet.

He leaned back in the chair and turned my way, obviously noticing my stare. "Hmm?"

"Nothing."

"You were staring at me pretty hard." He talked quietly so this mother wouldn't stir.

"Because you're handsome." I ran my hand up his arm, feeling the muscles of his powerful physique.

The corner of his mouth rose in an involuntary smile. "That's a very good reason." He set the book on the table beside him and rested his arms on the armrest. Like a draft of melancholy swept over the balcony, Calloway turned to the garden outside.

"Are you sure Jackson wouldn't come and visit?" Having another son present could pull Theresa out of her memory loss. Sometimes the most unpredictable stimuli could make all the difference in the world.

He rested his fingertips against his chin, where the stubble was thick. "Yes."

"Have you asked him lately?"

"I've asked him more than once," he said coldly. "He wants nothing to do with this. Says she's dead in his eyes."

That was the harshest thing I'd ever heard. "But she's not dead. You can still talk to her and enjoy spending time with her. Most of the conversations are repetitive, but she's still here. That's a very selfish thing to say."

"My brother is a very selfish man."

If I had loving parents the way Calloway did, I'd be there all the time too. I wouldn't turn my back on them. "I need to talk to him."

He chuckled like I made a joke.

"I'm serious."

"Sweetheart, we shouldn't waste our time. Jackson is who he is. I accepted it a long time ago."

"Well, I don't accept it. This is his mother too."

He shook his head. "I don't like being around Jackson any more than I have to anyway. So not seeing him works just fine for me."

"It's not about you. It's about her."

He didn't continue the argument even though it was obvious he still didn't agree with me. "I hate to say it, but I don't think we're making any progress. I think my mother's symptoms are permanent, and there's simply nothing we can do to change that. I'll always come visit my mother, but devoting so much time to seeing her every day is excessive. We should spend our time elsewhere — preferably in the bedroom."

We'd been doing this for weeks, and there was no change. I didn't want to throw in the towel, but it wasn't looking optimistic. "Let's give it a little more time…"

Calloway sighed when he didn't get his way, but he didn't press an argument. "A little more time. But that's it."

---

I rolled down the center divider in the car.

Calloway raised an eyebrow at my action.

"Tom, can you take us to Ruin?" I asked from the back seat.

Calloway narrowed his eyes at me. "What are you doing?"

Tom didn't obey my command the way he obeyed Calloway. I wasn't signing his checks, so I couldn't be that offended. "Sir?"

"We aren't going to Ruin," Calloway said calmly. "Take us home." He hit the divider button.

I hit the button again. "Calloway, I want to go to Ruin."

"To talk to Jackson?" he asked. "You can always call him if you want to speak to him that much."

"This is your mother," I argued. "I want to speak to him in person."

He turned his gaze out the window. "No. That's final."

I stared at him in shock, my eyebrows raised. "No?"

"Yes. No."

"You don't tell me what to do, Calloway. If I want to speak to Jackson, I will."

He turned back to me, his gaze just as fierce. "You don't speak to my brother about my mother. That's my business, not yours."

Now we were at an intense standoff. Our eyes were locked, and Calloway was bristling with anger. He wasn't going to back down, but I sure as hell wasn't either. We had just pulled up to a stoplight, so I opened the door and stepped out.

If only I could have seen the look on his face.

I stepped onto the sidewalk and started walking.

Calloway popped out of the car so fast it was terrifying. "Get your ass back in the car." He slammed the back door and immediately walked around the vehicle, right in front of the taxi that was sitting in traffic behind us.

I kept walking. "I'm going to Ruin even if I have to walk."

"I'd like to see you try." He caught up to me and grabbed me by the arm. His grip was tight as he yanked me back into him. The soft and affectionate look I was accustomed to seeing was now nonexistent. He looked frightening, his eyes scorching with lava. "Are you trying to piss me off?"

"Don't tell me what to do."

"I'll boss you around all I like when you cross a line. You aren't talking to my brother, and you certainly aren't walking there."

"I have legs," I said like a smartass. "And they work."

He gripped me harder, but he wouldn't cross a line with his strength. He applied the pressure but not enough to actually hurt me.

"Let me go of me."

His fingers dug into my skin. "We're going home, Rome. I'll throw you over my shoulder if I have to."

"I'm not your sub." I twisted my arm out of his grasp. "Don't treat me like one."

He dropped his hand, and the insult crept on to his features.

I knew that was low and I shouldn't have said it. Reminding him of what he couldn't have was just mean.

Calloway stepped back like he wanted to walk away, but his commitment to protecting me kept him on the sidewalk. He looked away with his jaw clenched, like he wanted to say a million things he would later regret.

Now I felt guilty for what I said. "I'm sorry…"

"For what?" he asked coldly. "For sticking your nose where it doesn't belong? Or for reminding me that I'm never going to get what I need? Which is it, Rome?" He turned back to me, his gaze bright with intensity. Tom had driven the car away during the argument because he couldn't stay sitting in the road.

"What you need? Or what you want?" I didn't know why I hovered over the choice of wording. Something about the violent way he spoke hit me in a painful way. I could hear the resentment, the disappointment.

"You're the biggest goddamn hypocrite I've ever met. You won't even consider giving me what I want when we both know you like it when I'm in charge. You like it when you slap me. You like the dark and kinky shit I'm into. So don't act like you don't know what I'm talking about."

"I'm not into—"

"Then you stick your nose in my family life when you have no right to do that. You won't even give me the courtesy of telling me who you really are, but you're just gonna storm into Ruin and talk to Jackson about my mom?"

My mouth opened to argue back, but I shut it again when I heard what he said. I didn't tell him who I really was? What did that mean? Did he know about my past? Or was he just making a general statement, and it was purely coincidence. I didn't see how it was possible that he could truly know anything about my abnormal past, so I assumed it was the latter.

Despite my rage, I understood why he was so upset. In the end, I knew I was the one at fault. I took a breath to calm myself and defuse the situation. We were alone on the corner, but within a second, a random person could pass by and watch our ridiculous fight. "You told me you would walk away from that life. I never asked you to, Calloway. So are you having doubts?"

He continued to give me a furious expression, his blue eyes resembling atomic bombs. He worked his jaw like his teeth were grinding together painfully.

His silence frightened me. "Calloway?" I felt my heart drop down into my stomach. I loved what we had, and I would be devastated if he wasn't happy. We'd grown so close to one another. It didn't even bother me that he didn't tell me he loved me since it was obvious every time he looked at me. "Calloway?"

He finally answered, his jaw still tense. "I've never doubted that I want to be with you—and only you."

A part of me wanted to read between the lines of his response, because he didn't truly answer the question. But a bigger part of me wanted to accept what he said instead of overanalyzing it. "What did you mean when you said I butt into your family's life but you don't really know who I am?"

He looked down the street like he may have been waiting for Tom to circle back and retrieve us. He was still tense with anger, his limbs shaking slightly because he was still so livid. Calloway was always intense, but this was a new level for him. "Nothing."

"Nothing?"

"You still have your walls up."

"I don't have any walls with you, Calloway." I'd allowed this man to become permanent. I relied on him for things I'd never relied on anyone for. I trusted him —loved him.

"There's more to your past that you aren't telling me about."

Was it a speculation or an accusation? I wanted to deflect the question altogether. "I don't see why my past matters. My life with you started the day I met you. Everything before that is irrelevant."

"You didn't tell me about Hank, and that mattered," he snapped.

The insult struck me like a palm to the face. "I thought I could handle it on my own —"

"And you couldn't. I could have removed that piece of shit a lot sooner."

I didn't like talking to Calloway like this. He was fearsome and irrational. He wasn't the man I knew, the one I'd fallen in love with. He was a beast that lost his temper. He could have yanked the stop sign out of the cement, and I wouldn't have been surprised. "I'm sorry about what I said. I was just upset and got carried away." An apology was always a good way to get the other person to calm down.

Judging by the cold way he stared at me, that wasn't enough.

"I was just trying to help with Jackson. But if you don't want me to talk to him, I won't. I just thought an outside perspective could change his mind. I admit Jackson is unreasonable sometimes, but if he's anything like you, I know he has a heart somewhere inside there."

"I've never seen it."

He was speaking out of anger, so I ignored it.

Tom pulled up to the curb in the black sedan, the windows tinted. He continued to stare forward so as to give us some form of privacy.

Calloway glanced at the car before he looked at me again.

I stepped closer to him and watched his body remain rigid. He usually softened when I came near, his arms automatically circling my waist and pulling me to his chest. I stopped in front of him and looked up at his fierce expression.

He didn't touch me.

I rose on my tiptoes and placed a kiss on his lips. His mouth didn't move and open for mine, but he didn't reject me either. My hands cupped his neck and used his frame for balance. When his lips were still unresponsive, I knew his anger couldn't be swayed with a simple kiss.

I pulled away, feeling defeated.

He suddenly grabbed me again and crushed his mouth to mine, his aggression skyrocketing from a standstill. The kiss was full of passion and anger, a mix of two emotions we'd felt before.

He abruptly pulled away as if he didn't trust our bodies when our lips were connected like that. "We'll go to Ruin and talk to Jackson." He walked around me and opened the back door.

"We really don't have to, Calloway…" I'd overstepped a boundary, and I knew it.

"Maybe you can talk more sense into him than I can." He extended his hand and waited for me to take it.

I eyed the hand that had touched me countless times. It had brought me joy and exquisite pleasure. I took it and felt the warmth encompass my palm immediately. "It wouldn't hurt, right?"

He kissed the top of my hand before he guided me inside. "No. It wouldn't."

---

Since it was earlier in the day, there weren't nearly as many people there. Women were still dressed in black leather with chains around their necks, but there were also a lot of women who looked ordinary. They weren't being bossed around like inferiors.

Calloway kept his arm tight around my waist as he guided me upstairs and to the back where the office was located. I'd been there once before, and everything looked exactly the same. The place was still black with lights that emitted a dull blue color.

He grabbed the handle and was about to walk inside when he realized his mistake. He raised his hand to the door, and after a breath, he knocked. "Jackson, it's Cal." He placed one hand in his pocket as he waited for a response.

"It's open," Jackson called.

We called inside to an interesting sight. Two women dressed in lingerie were making out on the couch, so absorbed in one another that they didn't even notice Calloway and me walk inside. Their tongues danced together as their hands explored one another.

I didn't know what my reaction should be. I'd never seen a sight like that before.

Jackson was behind his desk with his feet on the surface. He wore an intense expression just the way his older brother did when he looked at me. "What's up, bro? You're here early." His eyes never left the women on the couch.

Calloway didn't look at them, either out of respect for me or because he wasn't interested. "Can we talk for a moment?"

"What are we doing now?" Jackson asked like a smartass.

Maybe this wasn't a good idea.

Calloway hid his annoyance. "Rome would like your attention—and you better give it to her." The threat was unmistakable even though he didn't raise his voice.

"Rome, huh?" He finally met his brother's look with

a smirk. "I have time for her." He snapped his fingers to capture the attention of the women. "Ladies, let's pick this up later. I'll meet you in playroom number five."

The girls broke apart from each other and walked out with their hands held together.

When they were gone, Jackson turned his attention back to me. "I've never done a threesome with my brother — but I'm open to it."

"Jackson." Calloway only had to say his name to get his point across.

Jackson liked to push the envelope, but he would only push it so far. Like a bratty child with a parent, he knew the boundaries. He didn't roll his eyes, but it was clear he wanted to. "What can I do for you, Rome?"

Calloway adjusted the chair for me and waited for me to sit.

I took a seat and watched Calloway move to the chair beside me.

Jackson smiled like he observed something interesting. "I'm a busy man, Rome. As you can see from my two friends…"

I wondered if Calloway had done the same sorts of things. I'd never considered it before. Before I came along, he probably participated in things more serious than just a Dom/sub relationship. He'd probably been with two women at once, maybe more. He'd probably had a lavish sex life that I couldn't fathom. I'd spent my life as a virgin until the right man came along.

Since I'd lost my train of thought, Calloway started the conversation. "We've been visiting Mom a lot lately."

The mention of their mother immediately changed Jackson's attitude. He was no longer the playful playboy. "Is she okay?"

"A few months ago, she kinda remembered Rome," Calloway explained. "She couldn't necessarily remember her name, but she did recognize her face. I talked to her doctor about it, and he encouraged us to see her every day to see if her condition would approve."

"You've been seeing her every day?" Jackson asked incredulously.

"Not every single day," I said. "But almost every day."

Jackson rubbed his chin just the way Calloway did. They looked a lot alike, but they had distinctly different features. Calloway had a hard jaw, and Jackson's was a little softer. "And has there been any change?"

"No," I answered. "We are going to try for a few more weeks and hope something changes. But I think it could help if you came along."

He tensed at the question like he'd been hoping it wouldn't arise.

I was sympathetic to his reaction, but only so much. "This is your mother we're talking about, Jackson. You should be there for her. She would be there for you."

"I'm not really the best person for this," Jackson said. "I'm not good at the talking thing. And Calloway will tell you I can barely read." He forced a laugh that sounded completely false.

"Calloway isn't the best person for this either," I argued. "But he does it because it's the right thing to do. Calloway shouldn't have to carry this burden alone. You should be in this together."

"I'm not trying to sound like an asshole, but our mom is gone." Jackson shrugged in apology. "She can't remember us. She can't remember Dad. She can't remember who the goddamn president is. It's pointless. I'm not going to go down there and read to her when she's not going to remember anything anyway. Why put ourselves through that? She's in an assisted-living facility for a reason. Besides, I don't want to see her like that."

"But what if seeing you helps her memory?" I countered.

"Best-case scenario, she does remember Calloway and me. We spend the afternoon together and bond and whatever. And then the next morning when she wakes up, she forgets everything all over again. I know I sound like a dick, but seriously, what's the point?"

I understood where he was coming from, even if it was harsh. "Because she's your mom, Jackson. She gave birth to you and raised you, in case you've forgotten. It shouldn't matter if she remembers you or not. I'm sure you've forgotten lots of wonderful things she's done for you, but that didn't stop her from taking care of you."

Jackson bowed his head like the insult had some sort of impact.

Calloway crossed his leg and rested his ankle on the opposite knee. His fingers were interlocked on his lap as he stared at his younger brother behind the desk, in the seat he used to occupy on a daily basis.

Jackson gave a better response. "I'll think about it, okay?"

That was the best I was going to get out of him. "Thank you."

Calloway turned to me, surprise in his eyes. He probably assumed Jackson would never change his mind.

I rose from the chair because I was eager to leave Ruin. The place only reminded me of the kind of man Calloway used to be. When I was trying to find the right man to settle down with, he was here with a chain around some woman's throat. I didn't like thinking about his past, especially when it changed my current opinion about him. It wasn't fair either. "We'll leave you to your friends…"

Calloway followed me out without saying goodbye to his brother. We left the office then walked down the hallway. His hand found mine instantly, the affection reminding everyone around us that we were committed to one another. "I didn't think you were going to change his mind."

"Well, I haven't changed his mind — not yet."

## CALLOWAY

I had an incredible dream that night.

I walked into the house after a long day at the office. I undid my tie as I walked through the door and popped open the top button on my collared shirt. Rome was sitting on the couch with her paperwork on the coffee table. Her heels were slipped off her feet and tucked neatly under the table.

I stood at the edge of the living room and stared her down.

She met my look with her usual feistiness. "How was your day?"

I wasn't in the mood for small talk. I wasn't in the mood to be equals. I just wanted to be in control. "Don't speak."

The feistiness stayed in her eyes, but she didn't open her mouth again, obeying me like the good submissive she was. She knew I was in the mood to be more than just her boyfriend. She knew I wanted to dominate.

"On your knees." I didn't need to tell her twice.

She moved to the floor and sat on her knees, her hands resting on her thighs. Defiance was in her eyes because she didn't want to obey me. But she listened to me anyway, knowing this was what I needed.

And that made me rock-hard.

I stripped off my jacket and tossed it on the ground. Then I moved to my shirt next, taking my time as I undid each button. Despite her discomfort, I made her wait. She would sit there as long as I wanted her to. Now she was the submissive, and she had a job to do.

I dropped my shirt then undid my belt. I felt the leather in my hands and pondered if I should spank her for no reason whatsoever. I liked striking her hard, making her cry and beg for more at the same time.

But I didn't.

I tossed the belt to the floor then undid my slacks. I dropped everything on the ground and kicked off my shoes. A metal leash appeared from nowhere, and I approached her with the open collar in my hands.

She eyed it with hesitance but didn't object.

Because she didn't have a choice. I was the one in charge. I closed it around her neck and rested the collar on her shoulders. The leash was in my hands, the cold metal quickly warming under my heated skin. "Up."

She rose to her feet, still in the dress she wore to work that morning.

I walked up the stairs with her in tow. I guided us to the playroom that didn't exist in my home. A stack of chains sat on the table, and I grabbed the one that would be perfect for what I wanted to do with her.

I leaned against the foot of the bed with the leash still in my grasp. "Undress. Eyes on the floor."

She averted her gaze and unzipped the back of her dress. She yielded all the power to me, this mighty queen laying down her armor and bowing to me. She removed her dress and let it slip to the floor. Her bra came next, revealing her gorgeous tits that I would soon be clamping. She peeled her panties off next and kicked them aside.

Seeing her submit made my hands clamp around the chain, my knuckles turning white. "Come here."

She walked to the bed, her gaze still on the ground because she'd never been told otherwise.

"On your stomach."

Completely naked, she crawled onto the bed and lay flat, the curve of her ass contrasting against her level back.

I grabbed the extra chains that I needed and clasped

her ankles together. Then I chained her arms behind her back and forced them to rest along the steep curve. She was bound and ready to be enjoyed.

I crawled on top of her with a throbbing cock. I kept one hand on the leash like she might try to run away. The lube was handy, so I squirted it into her ass then massaged the small hole with my fingers. She was tense in anticipation, knowing my cock felt even bigger in her asshole.

My cock ached to be inside her as the minutes passed. My fingers felt her hole slowly loosen, growing used to the intrusion in the rear. Her breathing was heavy and irregular, sometimes aroused and sometimes frightened.

When she was loose enough, I shoved my huge dick inside her and stretched her unexpectedly.

She moaned when she felt the fullness in her back entrance, her moan mixed with a cry of pain.

"You know the safe word." She had the power to get out of this anytime she wanted. But she never uttered the word because she wanted me to enjoy the fun. She wanted me to get what I needed. Every time I did, I could go longer periods without having it. It worked in her favor.

I yanked on the chain and forced her chin back, my cock buried deep inside her. "Beg me to fuck you hard."

I tugged on the leash until her face was nearly pointed to the ceiling. She gasped for air because she could hardly breathe.

"Please...fuck me in the ass."

I released the chain and pounded into her hard, fucking her ass like a toy. I rocked the bed and banged the headboard against the wall. With every tap, I fell deeper into the moment. My woman was completely submissive to me, doing anything I asked without asking a single question. She let me do incredible things to her, allowed me to have complete control over her.

It was the greatest turn-on of my life.

I couldn't last long, not when my fantasy was coming true. I listened to her release moans that were quickly followed by cries because I was fucking her so hard. She enjoyed it, but it hurt at the same time.

I couldn't last any longer. I came with a moan.

And that's when I woke up.

My eyes popped open, and I saw the dark ceiling. My cock twitched as I came under the sheets, my come landing on my stomach. My body immediately jerked, and an uncontrollable moan escaped my mouth. I was half asleep so I couldn't think clearly. My hand wrapped around my cock, and I jerked myself as I finished.

Oh, fuck...

I stared at the ceiling as I caught my breath, still high from the incredible orgasm that shook me to the bone. It took me a moment to realize exactly where I was and who I was with. Rome was fast asleep beside me, having no idea what just happened.

Like a teenager, I had a wet dream.

Jesus Christ.

I kicked off the sheets then cleaned myself off in the bathroom. There was so much come I didn't know how I produced it all through a lucid dream. The door was shut and the light was still off, so I gripped the counter and leaned against, the images of the dream still faint in my mind.

I came hard with Rome—but not like that.

I was dreaming about the woman who was already in my bed, about the things I wasn't allowed to do with her. I thought I could defeat this, ignore my instincts, but perhaps that was wishful thinking.

Maybe I could never conquer this.

I wasn't betraying Rome because all of my fantasies were about her. But when she asked if I had doubts about our relationship, I gave her a sugarcoated answer —just the way she did to me. We both had our secrets from one another, but all couples did, right?

I walked back into the bedroom and got under the sheets, still smelling a hint of my seed stuck in the fabric. Hopefully, she wouldn't notice because she was used to the smell at this point.

I turned my head and glanced in her direction, relieved that she was still dead asleep beside me. Her face was beautiful when she slept, in the midst of peaceful dreams. She had no idea what kinds of thoughts existed in my mind. We saw two women making out for Jackson's enjoyment, and that didn't surprise me at all. Rome, on the other hand, wasn't sure how she should react.

Now that I was wide awake, I couldn't fall back asleep. My body was still hot from that dream I'd had, so erotic and dark. I'd give anything to do that to Rome in real life, to have her submit to me with a simple command.

Maybe there was a way I could still make that happen.

I had a phone meeting with a donor on the other side of the world, so I took the call while Rome prepared dinner in the kitchen. I could smell the shrimp on the stove along with the vegetables and rice. She didn't need to pay her portion of the mortgage because she definitely compensated in other ways.

I ended the call just in time to eat. The plates were on the table along with two glasses of wine. I sat across from her and enjoyed my dinner like I did every night, feeling like a married couple rather than something less serious. But the comparison didn't bother me. The idea of forever with this woman excited me rather than terrified me.

"How'd the call go?"

"Good. I got him to pledge a lot of money."

"How do you do that?" She swirled her wine before she sipped it. "To get people to hand over cash like that?"

"I'm pretty charming." My mouth stretched into an arrogant smirk so she knew I was kidding.

"You are very charming. Where did you learn?"

"It's not something you can learn. It's something you just have."

"I guess that would explain why Jackson's a shithead."

I chuckled before I drank my wine. "Great insight." I took a few bites and liked the flavor. Rome knew how to mix things together without making anything overly potent.

She stirred her rice around before she finally took a few bites. She chewed slowly then straightened her posture in the chair, as if she was preparing to say something. "Can I ask you something personal? Something you probably don't want to talk about?"

Even if I didn't want to talk about it, she could still ask me anything. "What's on your mind?"

"I was thinking about what I saw in Jackson's office the other day..."

The two women?

"I know you've been a Dom for most of your life."

All of my life.

"But...have you ever done other things?"

"Such as?"

"Like...been with two women at once?"

I was surprised she asked the question since the answer was pretty obvious. "Why do you ask?"

"I just...I'm not sure why. I know I don't really want to know these things. What you've done doesn't change where we are now. I guess I'm just curious, and I know curiosity killed the cat."

"Do you want me to answer your question?"

She took a few more bites as she considered the question. Then she dabbed her pretty lips with the napkin. "Yes, I do."

The question wasn't difficult to answer. "Many times."

Her expression didn't change into one of disappointment. She'd obviously been expecting it.

"Did you ever do things where you weren't the Dom?"

It wasn't something that could easily be turned off. It was a part of who I was. It was why I struggled to deal with her bossiness sometimes. My anger got the best of me, and I blew up when I shouldn't. "Other than with you, never."

"And a woman has never asked for more?"

Not even Isabella. All she wanted was to be my sub again. "No. I made my intentions very clear. Besides, women prefer me as a Dom."

"All the time?"

I nodded, knowing Isabella couldn't get enough of it.

She still seemed skeptical of that. She eyed me with hesitance before she took another bite of her food.

My hand automatically formed a fist on the table, my inner Dom clawing to the surface. I wanted to command her to get on her knees and suck me off until she choked. I wanted to tell her I would be her Dom whether she liked it or not. If she tried to run, I'd just chain her up.

"Everything okay?"

Rome's sweet voice forced my hand to relax. I eyed the food in front of me, reminding myself how happy I was just to have dinner with her. This sensation came at the most unexpected times. In general, I was happy and satisfied. I learned that I enjoyed making love when it came to the right woman. I enjoyed holding her while we slept together every night. I enjoyed everything about what we had.

But I would always want more.

---

I'd considered my plan several times and knew it wasn't solid. Rome could react in many different ways. She could tell me I had a serious problem and our relationship would never work. Or she could be tempted by the dark side and join me.

I wouldn't know until I tried.

I waited a few hours after dinner before I mentioned it. She was already in one of my long t-shirts as she sat on the couch, her hair pulled over one shoulder and her eyes on the TV. In a few hours, we would make love then go to bed.

But I had other plans.

I grabbed the remote and turned off the TV.

Rome eyed me, knowing it was too early for bed so I must want to say something.

"There's something I want to show you." I rose from the couch and grabbed my keys from the entryway. "I don't want to answer a million questions. I just want you to give me a chance and trust me." I inserted my hands into the front pockets of my jeans.

Rome's expression didn't change, but she was definitely caught by surprise. She watched me by the door until she rose to her feet. She looked at the ground as she considered the request. Her feet guided her to the stairway adjacent to the entryway. When she looked at me, the hesitance thudded in her eyes like a bright light. But she must have taken my words to heart because she said, "Let me get dressed."

---

I drove us to the private parking area in the back of Ruin.

The second we pulled into the spot and I turned off the engine, she knew where we were. She eyed the building before she turned back to me, disappointment written all over her features. She was a smart girl and had connected the dots instantly. A quiet sigh escaped her lips, loud enough that I could hear it in the car.

"Trust me." I knew she could ask me to take her home at any moment. If she did, I would have to do as she asked. I was a Dom who wanted to be obeyed, but strangely enough, I wanted her to have the power. The second she wanted something, I would give it to her—even if I didn't agree with it.

When she didn't speak, I knew she was trying to keep an open mind.

We walked to the back entrance where I used my key card and code to get inside. My arm immediately shot around her waist as I guided her through the crowded club. Music blared overhead, and couples paired off together on the dance floor.

I guided her upstairs to the playroom and located the one I'd specifically reserved for the evening. I slid my key card inside, and the room opened to a small area with a leather sofa. It faced a glass window that looked directly into a playroom, which was fully furnished with everything a consensual Dom/sub encounter could need.

Rome eyed the room, not having a clue what we were doing.

I grabbed her hand and guided her to the sofa. We both sat down, and I held her hand on my thigh.

We looked into the empty playroom.

Rome was patient for several minutes, not saying anything as she expected something to happen. But eventually, she grew tired of the unknown. "Calloway—"

The door to the playroom opened, and a man and a

woman walked inside. Jet was a good-looking guy with a powerful body, a fierce expression, and experience in the lifestyle that made him a respected Dom. With him was a woman who had been one of his favorite subs over the past year.

"On your knees." Jet issued the command with ease and pulled his shirt over his head, revealing a chiseled physique similar to mine. He gave her directions of what to do, having her behave in the exact manner he preferred.

I explained what we were doing. "They know we're here. But they can't see us."

"And why are we here?" She spoke quietly like we could be overheard.

"I want you to see what it's like, sweetheart. You won't give me a chance yourself. But maybe if you watched, you would understand."

A quiet sigh escaped her lips, her disappointment evident. "Calloway—"

"Just consider it. I'm not asking you to do anything but watch."

"I'm not gonna watch two people have sex," she argued.

"You've never seen porn?" I challenged, knowing even an innocent virgin like her must have touched herself to a good video every now and then. "It's not any different. In fact, they want to be watched. It's a fetish of theirs."

"It's still—"

"Rome, I'm asking you to do this for me. Isn't that enough?" I'd made a lot of compromises for her. It wasn't out of the question for me to ask her to do this in exchange.

Her eyes were glued to Jet and Jasmine through the window. Rome was obviously uncomfortable with them getting undressed, but once she relaxed, she would feel aroused. She would want what they had— but with me.

Jet stood naked at the foot of the mattress and looked down at Cynthia. "Suck me off. Now."

Her hands were in front of her with a sash, and she rose up to put his dick in her mouth. Jet gripped the back of her head and forcefully pulled her mouth over his length, hitting her in the back of the throat as he fucked her hard. Saliva dripped down her jaw and splashed onto her knees. She breathed whenever she had a chance but committed herself to sucking him just the way he wanted.

Jet played with his balls as he shoved his cock deep inside her throat, nearly making her gag a few times. When he was about to come, he pulled her mouth off his length and gripped her by the hair. "Hands in the air. Now."

She lifted her arms to the ceiling.

Jet fastened the shackles above her to her arms then suspended her inches above the floor. He snatched a whip from the stand then slapped her unexpectedly on the ass.

She cried out as she swung forward, her ass already marked red.

Rome immediately looked agitated, like she couldn't handle it.

I gripped her thigh and kept her steady. "Give it a chance."

"You want me to whip you, baby?" Jet asked as he positioned himself behind her, his cock still long and hard.

"Yes," she answered.

"You're gonna have to be louder than that."

"Yes," she yelled.

"You've been a bad girl, huh?" Jet came up behind her and gripped her by the hips. He kneeled down and kissed the area between her cheeks, licking her pussy as the whip remained in his hand.

She rolled her head back, her face tilted to the ceiling. "Yes..."

Jet ate her out for a few moments, worshiping her

body with his tongue. He sucked and licked, bringing her to the edge of bliss.

I eyed Rome out of the corner of my eye, hoping for some reaction. Her cheeks were slightly tinted, but I wasn't certain what that meant.

Jet stepped back with the whip. "You'll come when I tell you to come." He struck the whip across her back, making her swing forward with the momentum.

"Oh…"

He whipped her again, pacing back and forth as he admired the red mark down her back. "Do you understand me?" He whipped her again.

"Yes…" She moaned as the tears bubbled in her eyes.

"Yes, Sir," he corrected. He whipped her again.

The arrangement continued until she received ten lashes. Her back was marked with the red lines, but they were superficial and would fade by the following morning. He moved his arm with ease, striking her far gentler than I had with some subs.

He stepped in front of her and wrapped her legs around his waist then shoved himself inside her, having an easy entry because she was soaked. "Baby…you feel so good right now." He fucked her hard as she hung from the ceiling, her hips grinding with him as they moved together. He sucked her nipples into his mouth and even bit them from time to time. Every time she seemed to be hurt, she was quickly reabsorbed back into the moment.

Watching him fuck her with such intensity reminded me of my passion for Rome. I wish I were fucking her like that at this very moment. I wasn't aroused by Jet or Cynthia. But I was turned on by the idea of having that kind of relationship with the woman right beside me.

My hand moved to her thigh, and I slowly slid up her dress, migrating to the apex of her thighs.

She turned to me, her lips parted like she'd been breathing heavier than usual. Her cheeks were rosy and her nipples hard through the top of her dress. I recognized that look from all the times I'd fucked her.

She was turned on.

I knew it.

I moved my mouth to hers and kissed her as we both listened to Jet fuck Cynthia into oblivion. My tongue moved into her mouth until it met hers. They danced together with desperation, our mutual arousal combining. My hand continued up her thigh until I felt the lace of her underwear. I stroked it gently until my fingers pulled it to the side and exposed her glistening sex. The second I touched her clit, I felt the moisture. I rubbed her gently before I turned aggressive, making her pant and moan for me. She may have been thinking about Jet and Cynthia a moment ago, but she was certainly thinking about me now.

I fingered her and rubbed my thumb against her clit as I continued to kiss her. My hard dick pressed against the inside of my jeans as he ached for release. I wanted to fuck her senseless right then and there. Feeling her arousal across my fingertips, knowing she was hot for the same reasons I was, was a fantasy come true.

I was finally getting what I wanted.

If only I had done this a long time ago.

Jet and Cynthia were now irrelevant to me. They did their part, and now they were forgettable. I was a much stronger Dom than Jet could ever be. If Rome was turned on by that, wait until she saw me in action.

I lifted her from the sofa and carried her out of the room, still kissing her as I moved across the hall and got one of the playrooms unlocked. The door shut behind us, and I dropped her on the bed. I practically ripped her dress as I got it off, needing her to be naked as quickly as possible.

She unclasped her bra for me to speed things along, and I yanked her panties off and spotted the sticky arousal that soaked the fabric. My jeans and shirt were gone, and now my hands started to shake. I could finally have her the way I wanted her. Now I didn't know what to do first.

But then I snapped into action.

I snatched a handful of cable ties. "Turn over."

She did as I asked.

A thrill ran through my body immediately, making me tingle and go numb. Seeing her obey was the sexiest thing I'd ever witnessed. She didn't fight me. She just listened.

Fuck, I wasn't going to last long.

I stuck her ass in the air then yanked her wrists to her knees. I secured the cable ties around both her wrists and ankles, keeping them together so she couldn't move. She looked stunning that way, a sub ready to be spanked.

I needed to punish her. She'd made me wait so long for this. My chest was about to explode from the anticipation.

I pressed my mouth to her entrance and tasted her, feeling her arousal all over my tongue. I sucked her clit and ate her out like she was a feast prepared just for me. Her moans echoed in the room, growing louder and louder until she was on the verge of coming. I purposely sucked her clit harder to bring her to the very edge.

Then I pulled away.

Her moans turned into a whimper of devastation.

My hand moved to her ass, and I rubbed her cheek, my cock ready to burst at the sight. In a few seconds, my palm was going to mark her fair skin, turning it red. The outline of my hand was going to be imprinted on her skin until the following morning. "You deserve to be punished, Rome. You've teased me for so long."

She breathed deeply as she felt my hand glide over her ass. Her hair stretched down her back in loose curls, contrasting against her white skin. She glanced at me over her shoulder, her lips still parted with arousal.

"You have a lot of making up to do." I smacked my palm against her ass hard, making her jolt forward with the momentum. The clapping sound echoed in the playroom, music to my ears. My cock twitched at the same time, eager to be inside that wet cunt.

She gave a yelp as she shifted forward, not expecting me to spank her like that. She held herself up on her arms and stiffened.

My hand wrapped around her hair, and I yanked her head back, making her look toward the ceiling. "Men like me don't wait, Rome." I spanked her harder, leaving a mark on her ass where my hand struck her.

She shifted forward again, her neck strained since I had a hold of her hair.

I rubbed her other cheek, ready to make it just as red as the other. My cock slid between her cheeks

237

because he desperately wanted to be inside her. I hadn't even fucked her yet, and I'd never been this hard-up, this excited. I raised my palm to strike her again.

"Don't." She fought against the cable ties that secured her wrists to her ankles. "Stop."

We hadn't established a safe word yet, but when a woman told me to stop, I stopped. I wanted to keep going—more than anything else in the fucking world. My cock wanted to ignore her protests and suffer the consequences later. But the decent man inside me took control. I undid both of the cable ties so she could be free.

She immediately moved away from me on the bed, covering her chest with her arms like she didn't want me to look at her. Tears were in her eyes, and she pulled her knees to her chest, hiding her figure even more.

It killed me.

Naturally, I wanted to wrap my arms around her and protect her from all of her fears. But there was nothing I could do when I was the one she was terrified of. I grabbed my boxers and jeans and pulled them on, not wanting her to know that I was still hard for her. It would take me at least half an hour to come down from the high she just gave me.

I sat on the other side of the bed and waited for her to speak first, giving her the opportunity to say whatever she needed to say. I was devastated she'd pulled away from me. Did I hit her too hard? Did I do something to frighten her? Didn't she trust me enough not to take her somewhere she couldn't handle? "Sweetheart, talk to me."

"Why do you enjoy hurting me so much?" Her voice was heavy with impending tears. They didn't fall from her eyes, but they were bubbling under the surface. "Why am I not enough for you? Why do we always come back here?"

That was too many questions for me to answer at once. "You liked watching Jet and Cynthia. I thought you would understand that the relationship is beautiful. It's passionate. It's sexy. I want that with you."

"I thought what we had was already beautiful…"

"It is," I said quietly. "And I do cherish what we have. I just want more sometimes. I thought if I showed you what it was like, you might feel differently. And you did. We can argue all you want, but you were soaked before I even touched you. Explain that to me, Rome."

She held her tongue.

"Rome," I pressed. "Don't deny it."

She opened her mouth to speak but closed it again. Minutes trickled by, but she still didn't say anything. "I did like it. I did think it was sexy. But when I was on the bed…and you were hitting me…it made me feel worthless. It made me feel weak. It made me feel like someone you could abuse because I'm inferior to you. And it reminds me of…a lot of things. The fact that you enjoy hurting me so much just breaks my heart." She sniffed, and a tear finally came loose.

Now I regretted bringing her here.

I scooted to her side of the bed and wrapped my arm around her. "It's more than that, Rome. It's about trust. It's about you allowing me to do these things. I would never truly hurt you. I would never give you more than you could take."

"But why does it have to be this way at all?" she whispered. "Why can't we just be a normal couple that makes love? Why can't we have rough sex sometimes? Why do we have to go to this dark and disturbing place? I love you, Calloway. I just want you."

I pulled her into my chest and pressed my lips to her hairline. I wanted to tell her I felt the same way, but I just couldn't do it. She'd been so patient with me, but I couldn't cross that line. "I'm sorry. I really think if we tried a few times, you would realize it's a beautiful relationship. It doesn't make you weak. It's the opposite, Rome. It will make both of us strong. We don't have to do it all the time—just sometimes."

"I don't want to do it at all, Calloway." Her tears stopped, and her voice became stern. "I'm sorry. I know this is something you want, but I just can't do it. It goes against everything I believe in, everything I stand for. A woman should never have to put up with a man laying a hand on her—"

"It's not like that. Don't paint me a woman-beater." I wasn't like Hank and knocked her around because she said something to piss me off. "I spanked you so you would feel good. If you really fell into the moment with me, you would feel that pleasure."

She shook her head like her answer would never change. "I don't want this, Calloway. If this is something you can't live without, then..." She couldn't finish the sentence because it was too painful. "I understand."

Experiencing the high, even for a moment, reminded me how much I loved being a Dom, how much I loved being in a playroom. But I knew I would never have the same experience with anyone else. "I can't live without you, sweetheart. You know that."

She finally looked at me, her eyes still wet.

I kissed the corner of her eye and sighed, disappointed this dream was taken away from me. But I'd tried to make it work between us. I'd tried to show her it was more pleasure than pain. But her past, her struggles, clouded her mind so much that she couldn't truly feel the exhilaration. "I'm sorry I brought you here. I'm sorry I pressured you." When I held her against my chest, I felt her melt like she always did. Instead of storming off and saying I was an asshole, she stuck by me. If she was willing to put up with my transgressions, I needed to put up with hers. Otherwise, we would lose each other.

And I couldn't survive that.

I kissed her temple. "Let's go home."

We didn't have sex for two days.

I could tell she wasn't ready for it. Every night when we went to bed, she purposely turned away from me, her body language telling me everything I needed to know. Whenever she kissed me, it was always quick and passionless, like if she gave me more affection than that, it could give me the wrong impression.

But honestly, I didn't really want to have sex either.

Which was a first for me.

After having my fantasy in my grasp and losing it, I was too devastated to want anything. I had Rome on the bed with her ass in the air, her hands tied to her ankles, and I had the luxury of spanking her so hard my palm left a mark.

And then it was taken away from me.

Just like that dream I had, the experience was absolutely incredible. I'd never felt more alive than I did in that moment with her, when she allowed me to do whatever I wanted. Knowing her pussy got wet for the same reasons my cock got hard was everything I wanted.

But that was over.

Now I didn't know what to do. I didn't know where to go from here. I could just walk away from Rome and pick up a sub in a few hours.

But, fuck, I didn't want another sub.

I didn't want another woman.

I only wanted her Rome.

So how did I rectify this? How did I fix this?

I didn't have a clue.

I was sitting at my desk in the office when Jackson called me. Perhaps he'd made a decision about my mom. I took the call and stared out the window. "What?"

"Geez, you're in a bad mood."

I let the insult roll off my shoulder. "What?"

"Are you a parrot now?"

My hand formed a fist. "You have something to tell me, asshole? If not, I have shit to do."

"Whoa, alright," Jackson said. "I heard through the grapevine you took Rome to Ruin a few nights ago. But you didn't stick around. What happened?"

Jet must have mentioned it. "I don't want to talk about it, Jackson. I'll talk to you later." I moved the phone to the base.

"Whoa, whoa. Hold on. Don't hang up on me."

The only reason why I put the phone back to my ear was because he was my brother.

He must have known I was still around because he spoke again. "I'm not being nosy—"

"Sure seems that way."

"Judging from your tone, it didn't work out."

It blew up in my face. I only got to spank her twice before the fun was over. "No."

"She just wasn't into it?"

"She was." I knew that much. Her pussy couldn't have been that wet for no reason at all. "But her beliefs hold her back."

"Her beliefs?"

"She thinks it's sexist and abusive. She thinks by allowing me to do that to her, she's accepting disrespect. Hank messed her up real bad, and I suspect there was even someone before that who screwed her up too. She doesn't trust me enough to go down this road." I sighed into the phone, unable to hide my sadness.

"That's too bad. I'm sorry, Cal."

I heard the sincerity in his voice. It wasn't very

often when he acted like a compassionate human being. It was a good color on him. "I know."

"What are you going to do, then?"

"Same thing as before." I would have to fight my urges and beat off from time to time when the temptation became too much. The rest of the time, I was happy.

"You've been doing that, and it's obviously not working."

"If you're suggesting I leave her, I can't do that."

"Because of Hank?" he asked.

"No." Because I couldn't live without her—plain and simple.

"I don't understand. I couldn't just turn it off, you know? I couldn't just change who I am."

"She satisfies me every night. It's just every now and then when I want something more extreme…I take care of it in other ways."

Jackson knew what I meant. "I don't know…that's a big sacrifice."

I didn't see any other way. "We broke up once before, and I was far more miserable than I am now. It's definitely the lesser of two evils."

"Maybe you can wait a few months and try again. Or maybe even longer than that."

She was too stubborn to change her mind. After the

sight of her tears, I never wanted to cause her pain again. I got so much pleasure out of smacking her ass, but so much depression when she cried afterward. "No. It's over."

Jackson was silent over the line, accepting my circumstance.

"Isabella came to my office about a month ago." I wasn't sure what possessed me to say that. I'd be lying if I said her words hadn't affected me. The Dom inside me had been coaxed to life, piqued by her offer.

"What'd she say?"

"She wanted me to be her Dom again."

"How is that new?"

"She said she wanted me to control her, tell her what to do. But we don't need to have sex. We don't even need to touch."

Jackson finally caught on. "It's not a bad idea. You can take your dominance out on Isabella. It's not cheating if you don't touch her or beat off to her."

"Yeah..." Something in my gut told me it was still wrong.

"You get the best of both worlds, right?" Jackson asked. "You get Rome and all the vanilla, boyfriend bullshit. And you can get what you need from Isabella, the stuff Rome refuses to give you. I think that's more than fair."

Rome would never go for it. "I don't know…"

"And she doesn't even need to know. If anything, it would be better for Rome. She would never have to worry about BDSM popping up again. It would be gone for good. And if she's not willing to give you what you need, then she shouldn't be surprised that you're getting it from somewhere else. I think it's totally fair."

The more Jackson sided with me, the more tempted I became. But no matter how strong my urge was, I could never assuage the guilt sitting inside my stomach. If she went to an ex for needs I couldn't fulfill, I wouldn't be happy about it. But then again, I would always give her what she needed, so that would never happen.

And she wasn't willing to go that far for me.

"You should go for it. It's not like Rome would find out anyway. Say you're helping out at Ruin a few nights a month. You know the code here. No one is going to spill your secret, not even Isabella."

I worked my jaw and rubbed my fingers across the stubble. "Have you thought more about Mom?" The fact that I was even considering this innately wrong idea made me feel like an asshole. I changed the subject to hide the pain in my stomach.

Jackson quickly changed his tune. "I don't know, man…"

I didn't push him either way. I wasn't good at persuading people like Rome.

"Seeing her like that just makes me feel like shit."

"I'm not a fan of it either." But I manned up and did it anyway.

"I hardly talk to people I know. What am I supposed to talk to her about?"

"She's a human being, Jackson," I countered. "She just lost her memory. It's not like she turned into a squirrel."

"But you still know what I mean, Cal. Don't act like you don't."

I rubbed my fingers across my chin and stared at the city outside my window. I gently shifted my chair from left to right with my foot on the ground. My mind wandered to my mother and then back to Rome. "Let me know what you decide."

"I already said I didn't want to do it."

"Well, I don't accept that answer, Jackson. So think about it some more." I dropped the phone on the base without taking my eyes off the view from my office. I had emails to write and phone calls to make, but now I didn't feel like lifting a finger.

I didn't feel like doing anything.

## 13

### ROME

I was still upset.

I wasn't necessarily mad at Calloway for what he did. I wasn't angry that he still wanted that kind of intense sexual relationship. If anything, I felt guilty that I couldn't give it to him. When I saw Jet and Cynthia going at it, it did turn me on. The way she wanted him so much, allowed him to possess her like that, really was a turn-on.

But I hated watching him hurt her.

I hate hearing the crack of the whip against her skin.

I hated seeing him have so much power over her.

I would never forget what it was like to have my freedom taken away, to have my life in the hands of someone else. Being at someone's mercy was the worst thing in the world, and I absolutely despised it. Even if

Calloway was the one holding the reins, it brought back so many painful memories.

Calloway would never understand.

When I ran away, I promised myself I would never allow anyone to treat me that way again. When I met Hank and he pulled his tricks, I fought back and never gave up. If I allowed Calloway to do this to me, I was afraid of the repercussions for my psyche.

I never allowed myself to be damaged goods, to let myself become swallowed in self-pity. I was a strong woman who didn't quit. I had to keep going, to remain positive until the very end.

But these conversations brought out the worst in me.

At the end of the workday, Calloway arrived at my office, silent with his announcement. It was difficult to tell if he was in a good mood or a bad mood at this time of day since he rarely said anything.

His silence was impossible to ignore, so I packed my things and walked out with him. The office seemed to be back to normal like it was before they found out Calloway and I were an item. We didn't hold hands or show affection at the office. Even in the elevator, Calloway kept his hands to himself.

We spent the drive home sitting on opposite sides of the car. Calloway looked out his window, and I looked out mine. We hadn't had sex in a few days, which was our new record. Even when I was on my period, that didn't hold him at bay. I was certain he was getting anxious, and I was anxious too. That first step was difficult to take, where we would move forward and forget about the last time we were naked together.

We walked inside the house, and I slipped off my heels by the door. They killed my feet every day, but they looked so good with everything I wore that I had to keep wearing them.

Calloway slipped off his jacket and hung it on the coatrack. He walked up behind me and rested his hands on my arm, gripping me gently.

I froze in place, forgetting to breathe.

He rested his forehead against the back of my head, his gentle breaths falling on the back of my neck. His fingers were callused against my skin, but they were warm and inviting. His touch was nothing like it was in the playroom at Ruin. This touch was gentle, full of affection, just the way I liked. "I need to make love to you." He pressed his lips against the back of my neck, a kiss as light as a feather.

A thrill immediately shot down my spine. My body came to life after the last two days of dormancy. Like he'd never hurt me, I suddenly craved him with urgency. The second his lips were on me, I felt that shot of ecstasy, the rush I only felt when he touched me.

I tilted my head back against his shoulder and exposed my neck, wanting more of his mouth on me.

He took the offering and kissed my neck and my jawline, his stubble rubbing against me as he devoured me. His kisses were slow and purposeful but full of undeniable passion. He squeezed me with his strong hands then wrapped his arms around my waist, pulling me into his chest as he kissed me harder.

Now I was desperate for his mouth on mine. My skin wanted more of his caresses, but my mouth was the one in charge. I craned my neck despite the discomfort and kissed him over my shoulder. He kissed me harder once he had my mouth. He yanked me into his body, pressing his hard cock right against my ass.

Like I'd never been upset at all, I wanted him more than I ever had.

We took our time getting up the stairs. Sometimes he pinned me against the wall in the hallway and kissed me because he was too impatient to wait until we reached the bedroom. Another article of clothing was removed and dropped to the floor, forming a trail throughout the house.

By the time we entered the bedroom, we were both naked and anxious. He got me on the bed with my back to the mattress. While he wasn't as carnal as he was the last time we fooled around, he was still aggressive and desperate. He made me feel wanted, desired. I was vanilla and I would always be vanilla, but he still craved the plain flavor.

He pinned my legs back with his arms behind my knees, opening me wide so he could enjoy me as thoroughly as possible. He held his massive frame above mine with the strength of his arms. He was a sight to behold, a man so sexy it was hard to believe.

The head of his cock found my entrance like it had a mind of its own. He stretched me wide apart, making my eyes sting with tears because I realized how much I'd missed his throbbing cock inside me.

He watched my eyes water but understood what the tears meant. He gave me his entire length then closed his eyes as he moaned, feeling the same surge of joy. His balls slapped against my ass with his initial thrust, hitting me hard right against my cheeks.

I dug my nails into his ass as I pulled him deep inside me, feeling the pleasure and discomfort his entire length caused. Sometimes I didn't understand his need to be so violent, to chain me up and slap my ass until I cried. I thought the sex we had was already incredible, already perfect. Could it really get better than this?

He dug one hand into my hair as he began to thrust

inside me, claiming my pussy as his all over again. His lips were just inches from mine, but he didn't kiss me, his warm breaths falling on my skin. I could hear his arousal with every breath he took, could feel his desperation for me every time he thrust inside me.

I wanted to come already, either because Calloway was that good or because it'd been two days since the last time we made love. Before he came along, I was just fine being single and saving myself for the right guy. But now that I'd been with Calloway, I was grouchy when I didn't get my fix. I was angry when I didn't get those blissful orgasms that Calloway handed out like candy. I turned into a spoiled brat who needed to always get her way.

I ran my hands down his chest and felt the sweat stick to my fingertips. His muscles tensed and shifted as he moved his body in the sexiest ways. His breathing was harsh with arousal, and the quiet moans he made as he thrust into me made my pussy tense automatically in response. I wanted to keep going for the rest of the night, but I wanted to come. If I did, Calloway wouldn't last much longer because the expression on my face usually triggered his orgasm. So I held off as long as I could to make it last.

"Let go." His words came out as a command. "I'll

make you come as many times as you want, sweetheart."

Calloway knew me better than I realized. He could read my mind and understand my body even better than I could. He gave me a hard kiss, full of tongue and passion, and pounded me into the bed so I would be forced to explode.

And I did.

I dug my nails into his back as I came around his cock, shaking with an explosion that gripped me by the throat. I screamed so loud I hurt my own ears. My pussy tightened around him as my come gushed all over his length, dripping down to his balls.

The pleasure was so good I became light-headed, floating above the clouds as I enjoyed the exquisite tenderness between my legs. The ecstasy compensated for the dry spell we went through, making up for the lack of physical bliss we deprived ourselves of over the past few days. "God, I love you…" I meant those words in many different ways, but each one was sincere. I loved him because he was a good man with a big heart. But I also loved how amazing he was when he was between my legs.

A quiet moan erupted from deep in the back of his throat, his ego obviously doubling in size. "Don't make me come, sweetheart. You know how much I want to."

He slowed his pace and rocked into me gently, moving through my slickness. He usually changed positions after he made me come the first time, but now he stayed on top of me, rocking me hard enough to make my tits shake up and down.

He leaned down and pressed his lips to mine, kissing me slowly, bringing my arousal back up to top speed after a few seductive minutes. He sucked my bottom lip into his mouth then rubbed his nose against mine, teasing me before his mouth was on mine once again.

God, he was hot.

He pinned my legs back farther then changed the angle, making his pelvic bone rub right against my nub. He applied the right kind of friction and made my clit throb with pleasure. My pussy somehow became even wetter, even tighter.

Calloway could sense the difference. "Your pussy is fucking incredible."

That was only because he was the sexiest man on the planet.

He increased his pace because he knew I was on the edge of another explosion. He was driving me home, getting me to the finish line so he could join me. "Show me that O, sweetheart."

I reacted on command, and I came all around him,

screaming again like the first orgasm never happened. I dug my fingers into arms and held on as the sensation rocked through me, burning hot like lightning just struck me. It was so good I wanted to cry, so powerful I wanted to collapse.

Calloway kept pounding into me as he approached his climax.

I pressed my hand against his chest and made a very selfish demand. "One more..." I was lucky enough that I had a man who could make me come at all, and I shouldn't take it for granted. But I was greedy after two days of nothing. I was so hard up I wasn't even sure why I stopped him from spanking me in the playroom. All the pain in the world would be worth having him inside me.

He clenched his jaw like he was annoyed that he had to restrain himself. His eyes bored into mine, their usual look of intensity shining bright. But he didn't release himself, somehow finding the strength to hold it together for a little longer. "What my woman wants, she gets."

---

"How did your date go?" I asked as I sat across from Christopher at the deli. He picked me up for lunch while Calloway's assistant picked up something for him. He was busy at the office, so he didn't have time to join us.

"She was so boring. Almost fell asleep."

"Almost fell asleep on a date?" I asked incredulously.

"Yep." He took a bite of his sandwich and chewed. "She was that boring, if you can believe it."

"Actually, I can't."

"She doesn't have friends or hobbies. She just goes to work and then goes home. She's hot as hell, but that's all she's got going for her."

"So when dinner was over, you just went home?"

"No." Christopher took another bite and scarfed down his food quickly. "We fucked, and then I went home."

I rolled my eyes.

"I told you she was hot."

"So she couldn't have been that boring."

"Well, there's no talking during sex, so it's pretty hard to be boring." He ripped open his bag of chips and put them on the table between us so we could share. "What's up with you and the Hulk?"

"The Hulk? He's not green."

"But he turns green when he's angry. I've seen him in action."

"Things are good…" I sipped my iced tea then dove my hand into the chip bag.

"Oh no." Christopher saw right through that. "What happened?"

I told him about the fiasco at Ruin.

"Rome, just do it. You can tell the guy is really into it."

"I know he is…but I don't want to."

"The guy wouldn't have made a move unless he thought you might be into it."

I didn't mention all the details about Jet and Cynthia. That was a little too awkward to talk about.

"He's given up a lot for you. I don't see why it's so difficult for you to do something for him—even if you don't like it."

"Do I really need to explain my reasoning?" I didn't want to repeat myself for the fifth time.

"Look, I get what you're saying. But relationships are about sacrifice, right?"

"But I'm not willing to sacrifice everything I believe in. I've been knocked around too many times in my lifetime. I don't want to go through it again just because my hot boyfriend is into weird shit."

"He wouldn't be knocking you around," Christopher corrected.

"Fine. He would whip me like an adulteress in the

middle of the town square," I said sarcastically. "Much better."

"Don't be a brat, alright? It's not like that either."

"You're only saying this because you're into weird shit too, Christopher."

"Maybe," he said in agreement. "But if you don't keep your man happy, he'll go looking for it elsewhere..."

The insinuation made me run cold.

"I'm not saying Cal is a cheater. Seems like a really honorable guy. But one day, he's gonna get frustrated and leave. That's how men are. We need a woman to keep us fed and keep us satisfied. If you do those two things, we won't go anywhere. We're very simple creatures."

Christopher said a lot of stupid things, but that wasn't one of them. When men didn't get what they needed, it was natural for them to look for it elsewhere. "But he is satisfied with me." I knew Calloway wanted to do those things sometimes, not all the time. If that were the case, we wouldn't have lasted this long.

"I'm sure he is—for now. Just think about it, Rome."

"I already have."

Christopher knew I could be just as stubborn as he was, so he dropped the subject. "How do you find a nice woman in this city? Someone who's super sexy but super awesome too. I'm not a big fan of online dating, so I haven't gone there."

"We're in New York. There are amazing women everywhere."

"Yeah, but I need a woman who's wife material."

"What's wife material?"

He took another bite as he considered the question. "I don't care if she's rich or poor, but I want her to be doing something with her life, you know? Be passionate about something."

"Again, lots of women meet that criteria."

"And she's gotta cook, and not just Top Ramen."

"That shouldn't be hard to do."

"And she's gotta be sexy, but not vain about it."

Most pretty women I knew were like that, so that might be difficult. "That might be a little hard to find."

"Well, I'd rather have a super awesome chick who's a six than a boring-ass chick who's a ten...so I guess looks are negotiable."

"You know what you should do?"

"Hmm?" he asked.

"Just go out and meet people. When you find the right woman, you'll know. Don't make a list and expect her to fit each criteria. Calloway doesn't fit all of my criteria, but that didn't stop me from falling in love with him."

"Well…he doesn't meet one extremely important item on your list. And it seems like it's been a recurring problem."

I didn't want to live without Calloway. My heart bled for him in ways it wouldn't bleed for anyone else. Being madly in love with him made me accept his flaws, no matter how disturbing they were. "We'll make it work. I don't know how, but we will."

"Maybe I can meet someone at Ruin. You know, a kinky chick."

I couldn't picture Christopher with any of the women there. If he wanted a wife, he needed someone who wasn't willing to have a chain around her neck. "I think you would have a good time but wouldn't want to settle down with her."

"Hmm…that's true."

We'd never talked extensively about Christopher's love life. Ever since he decided he wanted to settle down and get married, that was all we ever talked about. Christopher didn't seem desperate, but he definitely seemed anxious. "When it's meant to happen, it'll happen."

"Hopefully. Just hope I didn't wait too long that all the good ones are gone."

"You haven't been out with anyone that you really liked?"

"Well..." He dug his hand into the chip bag. "There was this one woman, Kim. She was pretty amazing. Beautiful, cool, she had the whole package. But I slept with her and never called her again...ignored her phone calls. She'd never give me another chance."

"How long ago was this?"

"Like...six months ago."

Yeah, she'd probably moved on by now. "Why did you blow her off?"

"I really liked the connection, but I was so anti-commitment that I didn't even bother. Since I wasn't looking for anything serious, I just tuned everything out. I didn't start thinking about how awesome she was until recently."

If it were me, I probably wouldn't give Christopher another chance. It would make me come off as a desperate, something I refused to do. If this Kim chick was anything worth chasing after, she was probably the same way. "Six months is a long time."

"Yeah, I'm pretty sure she's long gone."

We ate the rest of our lunch in silence until every single piece of food was long gone. Christopher eyed his watch like he needed to get back to work soon. "I'll walk you back to the office and head on my way."

"I don't need you to walk me, Christopher. Hank is no longer a problem." In fact, he was a complete pussy.

"I know Cal. He'd be ticked if I let you walk on your own."

"You guys both need to accept the fact that I'm perfectly safe now. Let's go back to normal." Christopher and I walked out of the deli and headed to my building a few blocks away. "And my building isn't even on your way."

"I could use the exercise." He walked with his hands in the pockets of his slacks.

"I still don't want things to be this way. I can't remember the last time I was alone—truly alone."

"No one likes being alone, so consider yourself lucky." He walked me until we reached the outside of my building. He looked up at the large floor-to-ceiling windows then raised his hand for a high five. "See you later, sis."

I smiled then smacked my palm against his. "Good luck with the ladies."

"I don't need any luck." He waggled his eyebrows. "But thanks."

# 14

## CALLOWAY

I tried to forget that terrible night and move on with my life.

Move on with Rome.

I made my peace with the fact nothing would change. She wasn't going to budge in her decision, as ridiculous as it was, and I had to accept it. As disappointed as I was, I knew I had to make this work because I'd be so much more miserable if I lost her.

Been there, done that.

I finished up in my office then walked down the hallway until I walked into her space. Rome sat at her computer desk with perfect posture, looking just as refreshed as she did when she walked in that morning. She was so passionate about her projects that she never seemed drained.

She didn't notice me because she was typing an email on her computer. She was so engrossed in what she was doing she didn't realize I was lurking in the doorway.

I let her finish before I made my presence known. "Ready to go, sweetheart?"

She nearly jumped out of her skin when she realized I was there. "Geez, how long have you been standing there?"

"For a few minutes. But don't feel bad. I enjoyed the view."

Her mouth automatically fell into a warm smile as she shut down her computer and grabbed her purse. "Of me sitting on my ass."

"Any view of that ass is a good one."

She met me by the door, and to my surprise, she stood on her tiptoes and kissed me on the lips. She never gave me affection at the office, but she must have made an exception since most of the staff were already gone for the day. Or I just looked so handsome that she didn't care.

I hoped it was the second one.

We left the office together then rode the elevator down to the ground floor. My hand found hers, and I intertwined our fingers, not caring if the security guys spotted us together. We were both off the clock, so the affection shouldn't matter. Plus, I was the boss. So, it really shouldn't matter.

"Wanna see my mom today?" We saw her almost every day. Sometimes it was for an early dinner or later in the evening before she went to bed.

"Yeah. Is Jackson coming?"

I was pretty sure that ship was never going to sail. "I don't think Jackson is gonna come along."

"Then you need to make him."

"It's impossible to make the Owens brothers do anything."

"We'll see about that." She extended her open palm and silently asked for my phone.

I fished it out of my pocket and dropped it into her hand.

She looked through my contacts then called him once we were sitting in the back of the car.

"Yo," Jackson said into the phone. "Sick of the same flavor yet?"

I knew exactly what he meant by that, and I was sure Rome did too.

If she did, she didn't make it apparent. "It's Rome, not Cal."

"Oh...what's up?" He immediately became

uncomfortable, probably knowing why she was calling before she even said anything.

"We're going to see your mother, and you're joining us."

"I'm busy," he barked. I could hear him from my seat against the window.

"Then stop being busy," she argued. "We're pulling up to Ruin, and you better come out."

"Or what?" he asked with a laugh.

"I'll march in there and pull your ass out, that's what." Rome's eyes turned that sexy green color they did when she was sassy.

Now I really wanted to fuck her.

Jackson didn't make the mistake of calling her out on her bluff. "Jesus Christ, fine. I'll be outside in ten minutes."

"Make it nine." She hung up and handed the phone back to me.

My cock was hard in my slacks and was eager for release from his cage. Oddly enough, I liked to be the one in charge, to tell people off and be an asshole. But when she ran the show and made the demands, it really turned me on. I still hadn't figured out why.

The driver changed direction to Ruin, and I rolled up the center divider between us. The back windows were tinted so we had all the privacy we needed. I was eager to get my dick inside her, the dominant version of me coming out when I didn't expect it to. I undid my slacks and pulled my cock out. "Suck me off. Now."

Her eyes widened imperceptibly when I issued the command.

Instead of backing off, I held my ground. I massaged my length with my hand, rubbing my thumb over the head where the small drop formed.

Witnessing me touch myself must have turned her on because she pulled her hair over one shoulder then leaned over me in the back seat. She grabbed my base then wrapped her lips around my length, taking me in just the way I liked.

I leaned back and watched her as my hand dug into her hair and fisted it so it wouldn't fall into her face. "We have about six minutes. Make it quick." I guided her face up and down, having her move across my length the way I preferred.

Rome did as I asked, moving down my length quickly without wasting any time. She jerked her hand at the same time, giving me a quickie that would have a satisfying climax at the end.

I yanked up her dress then gripped her backside with my free hand, loving the perky curve of that ass. I spanked her gently, my instincts kicking in.

She didn't stop what she was doing. In fact, she

moved harder. Saliva dripped down my length to my balls, and she made quiet gagging noises when she took too much of my cock into that tiny little mouth. She forced her jaw apart so her teeth wouldn't nick me. For someone so inexperienced, she gave great head.

When she moved to the top of my head, she sucked it hard, pulling all the pre-come from my head onto her tongue, and then sheathed me once more. Without sticking my hands between her legs, I knew she was wet.

I knew we were just a short distance away from Ruin, but I wouldn't last much longer anyway. I ran my hand over her ass and the steep curve in her back, feeling the searing heat deep in my groin.

"Faster."

Rome craned her neck and moved up and down faster, some strands of hair falling toward her face. She breathed through her nose and flattened her tongue, giving me a good and hard blow job.

I was about to come. I felt it all the way in my bones. "It's coming, sweetheart."

She deep-throated me harder even though it caused tears to sting her eyes.

That was my woman. She wanted to give it to me good no matter how uncomfortable it made her.

She massaged my balls as she took more of my cock, wanting my come as desperately as I wanted to give it.

I knew the finale was here. It burned me from the inside out because it was so powerful. I grabbed the back of her neck and guided her along my length exactly the way I wanted. When my cock thickened and I released, I pushed her mouth down completely on my length so she would get every drop right down her throat. "Fuck...yeah." I laid my head back and closed my eyes, enjoying her wet mouth still tight around my cock. My balls tightened in joy as they released.

Rome took everything without gagging, devouring my come like a pro. She never complained about my size or the amount of seed I dumped inside her. She did the best she could because I always did the same for her.

She pulled my cock out of her mouth then licked her lips. Webs of saliva extended from her lip to her chin, so she grabbed a tissue and cleaned herself up. The back of the car immediately smelled like a mixture of come and saliva, but that didn't matter because I owned the damn thing.

I cleaned up and pulled my boxers and slacks back on.

Rome sat beside me and crossed her legs like

nothing had just happened. She returned to looking like a graceful lady, poised and refined.

She was definitely the queen of great head.

The car came to a stop, and when I glanced out the window, I realized we were in front of Ruin. "Right on time."

She fixed her hair then gave me a seductive smile. "I get the job done."

I chuckled and pulled her into my side for a kiss. The need for affection overcame me, and I yanked her right beside me so I could treasure her. Moments like this made me realize not getting what I wanted wasn't the worst thing in the world. Even though she wasn't a sub, she went the extra mile to please me. She was beautiful, absolutely wonderful. I couldn't whip her or suspend her from the ceiling, but I got just as many good benefits from our relationship. She was definitely the sexiest woman I'd ever been with. Even when we were screwing, I enjoyed being around her. I'd never felt that way for any other woman.

We walked inside and entered the office where Jackson was likely hiding. Instead of knocking, we just walked inside and spotted him sitting at his desk.

He sighed when he spotted us. "Am I being kidnapped?"

"Yep." Rome stepped forward, her hands on her

hips. "Are we gonna do this the easy way or the hard way?"

"Depends," Jackson replied. "Does the hard way involve you touching me?" He smiled like an arrogant asshole.

I gave him a warning with just my eyes.

"Actually, yes." Rome approached the desk. "It involves my foot right against your dick."

"Like...you'll jerk me off with your feet?" he asked hopefully.

"Jackson." I gave him his second warning. He knew what would happen if I had to warn him again.

"You guys are so lame." He rolled his eyes then hopped out of the leather chair. "Fine, whatever. Let's get this over with."

---

Jackson trailed behind and practically dragged his feet on the ground. He hung in the rear as we moved through the assisted-living facility and to my mother's room. We greeted the nurse then walked inside. The French doors that led to the patio were wide open, and my mother sat in the lounge chair with her knitting on the table beside her.

Jackson stopped in the middle of the room, his feet

suddenly immobile. He stared at the back of our mother's head, a reluctant expression on his face. He looked frozen, even scared.

I'd never seen him make a face like that.

Jackson continued to stare at her, watching her hands work the fabric of the scarf she was making. He suddenly looked like a little boy again, a small child who longed to be in the protective arms of his mother.

Rome went ahead first and greeted my mother. Their quiet voices barely trailed to our ears inside the apartment.

I walked back to Jackson and stood beside him. "You can do it, man."

"I haven't seen her in…years."

"I know." Jackson was one of the few people in the world where I could let my guard down. He said a lot of stupid things to piss me off and did even stupider things to make me angry. But all of that didn't matter because he was still my brother. "It'll be okay. You don't have to say anything."

"I'm not sure if I could even if I wanted to…"

I wanted to tell him it got easier as time went on, but it never did. Seeing my mother so weak and helpless was always heartbreaking. She used to be strong, the kind of woman that didn't put up with anything. She spent her time gardening, getting her hands dirty in the soil, and the house was always spotless. If I came home from school and trailed mud into the house, she would make me mop and vacuum the entire house just to teach me a lesson. I thought she was a hard-ass at the time, but now I understood she made me into a strong man rather than an arrogant asshole. "It'll be alright. She's a delight to talk to."

"Yeah?"

I nodded then patted him on the back. "Come on."

I walked onto the balcony next, watching Rome and my mother chat about the new flowers that had just been planted in the garden over the balcony. I held the book under my arm and greeted her with a smile. "You must be Theresa. I'm Calloway." I extended my hand.

She eyed it before she shook it.

It was strange to shake hands with my mother. It never got easier.

"You're a very handsome young man." She usually blurted that out at some point during the conversation.

"Thank you. You're a very pretty lady."

She immediately smiled at the compliment. "That's very nice of you to say."

I moved aside so Jackson could greet her.

He stepped closer then eyed her blankly, at a loss of words now that he was face-to-face with our mom. It'd been at least five years since he last saw her face.

275

Mom stared at him blankly, obviously uneasy about the odd way he was looking at her.

Suddenly, Jackson kneeled down and hugged her. He wrapped his large arms around her and held her. "I'm Jackson..."

My expression softened when I saw Jackson wear his heart on his sleeve. He acted like a tough guy all the time, but he was just a man underneath that rough exterior.

Mom returned the embrace, and a small smile crept on to her lips. "You're a very sweet young man. It's nice to meet you."

Rome blinked her eyes quickly to rid her tears.

Jackson finally pulled away, looking just ghostly as he did before. "Thanks..." He rose to his feet again then stood beside me like he didn't know what else to do.

We took our seats in the lounge chairs, looking at my mother with the partially completed scarf on her lap. Her short hair was curled and framed around her face. She wore a blue collared shirt with a white gold necklace around her throat. Her eyes were alive with brightness now that she had company to share the afternoon with. I could see so many of my own features, my eyes as well as my facial structure. I'd inherited my father's rugged masculinity, as had Jackson. But the few soft expressions I possessed came from her. "We thought we could read to you today. How does that sound?"

"That's very sweet, but no thanks. I would much rather enjoy a conversation with you." My mother's reaction to us was always different, and that was interesting to both Rome and me. Sometimes she wasn't in the mood to talk. All she wanted was to listen to a good story. And other times, she wanted to chitchat. Her moods couldn't be attributed to any specific event. That was just how she felt when she woke up first thing in the morning.

She eyed Jackson and me, her gaze switching back and forth between us. "Are you two brothers? You have the same eyes…"

Jackson was still incapacitated. Words didn't form on his tongue, and he didn't open his mouth to speak.

So I took over. "Yes, we are. I'm the older one."

"That's sweet," she said. "You guys are close?"

That was a complicated question. "We see each other pretty often." We didn't exactly go out and get a beer together, but we seemed to be in each other's business a lot.

She nodded. "That's lovely." She turned to Rome. "Are you seeing either one of them?"

Rome placed her hand on mine. "Calloway and I have been seeing each other for almost a year."

Wow. I couldn't believe how much time had passed. "Yeah."

"Do you have a girlfriend?" Mom asked Jackson.

"Uh…" Jackson struggled to answer the question even though her interest seemed harmless. "No…no girlfriend."

"Take your time," Mom said. "You want to find a nice girl to settle down with. It's better to wait for a truly fantastic woman than to settle for someone mediocre. You two are too handsome for ordinary."

My mom still gave me advice without even realizing it.

"Keep waiting, Jackson," Mom continued. "I'm sure there's another Rome out there for you."

Rome smiled at the compliment.

Jackson still looked sick.

I nudged him in the side, encouraging him to talk to her like she was a normal person.

Jackson cleared his throat. "So…what are you making?"

"A scarf." She held up the piece she'd constructed. It was only halfway completed, but it was a nice mixture of colors, perfect for springtime. "I'm not sure if I'll ever wear this, but I thought it would look nice."

"Yeah…" Jackson cleared his throat. "It is nice."

I knew I couldn't push Jackson too hard. He wasn't

good at dealing with his emotions. I wasn't much better, but I could handle difficult situations a little better. "Maybe you could wear it with a dress or something."

"Exactly what I was thinking." She eyed Rome before she turned back to her knitting. "But I think Rome would look much better in it. Just let me finish this up, and you can take it with you when you go."

"Oh…" Rome flinched at the offering. "Thank you…that's sweet."

"A beautiful scarf for a beautiful girl," Mom said. "It's perfect."

Rome smiled, her eyes full of tears.

Even when my mother didn't know who we were, she still treated us exactly the same way as she would if she knew Jackson and I were her sons. That was the kind of person my mom was, always making everyone feel like family. My dad was such an ass to her. I was grateful she didn't remember him.

Jackson must have had the same thought because he suddenly excused himself to use the restroom. "I'll be right back…" He left the patio and retreated back inside.

Rome watched him go, sympathy written on her face.

I decided to follow him, knowing he needed some comfort in this dark time. Rome engaged my mom in conversation, so I slipped away without notice. I walked inside and reached the lobby where Jackson had taken a seat on one of the comfortable couches.

I sat right beside him, our knees almost touching.

Jackson stared at the floor. "Sorry…I just…I don't know."

"I get it, man."

"She's exactly the same, you know? She just doesn't remember things."

"Yeah, her personality hasn't changed."

"I feel like I'm talking to my mom…but she doesn't know I'm her son…but I feel like her son."

I nodded. "I get what you're saying."

"Makes me happy, but it also makes me sad."

Those were the exact emotions I felt every single time I came to visit. "I want to tell you it gets easier, but it doesn't. I guess I've gotten a little numb now that I've been visiting her more often, but even then, it's not easy seeing her like this. But you know if the situation were reversed, she'd visit us every single day."

Jackson showed his agreement with a nod. "Yeah… now I feel guilty."

He should have been visiting her with me this entire time, but I certainly didn't think less of him for it. "Don't feel guilty. I know your absence isn't caused by indifference, but pain."

He finally pulled his gaze from the floor and stared straight ahead. "Rome is good with her."

"Rome has a special effect on people." She'd worked her magic the first time I laid eyes on her. After all this time, I was still just as obsessed as I was then. "Mom never remembers her, but she always falls in love with her every time she comes to visit."

"Yeah, I can see why you've fallen in love with her."

I didn't agree with the statement, but I didn't contradict it either. Love was a complicated emotion that was too pure for me to feel. My father claimed he loved my mother, and then he turned into a complete nightmare.

"I guess I can go back in there now. Just needed a moment to calm down. This is a lot harder than I expected it to be."

"Just remember, Mom is in a great place. This facility takes good care of her, cooks for her, takes care of her medications. She's in great health too. She does her hair just the way she used to, wears nice clothes… she's the same."

"Yeah, I know."

I patted him on the shoulder. "Let's get back in there. Visiting hours are over in about an hour."

"Okay." He took a moment to compose himself before he stood up, rising to his full height. He nearly as

281

tall as I was, only about an inch of difference between us. "Let's do this."

We finally made it home and had dinner. We were both starving after spending the evening with my mother and having nothing in between. We ate at the dinner table like usual but didn't make conversation because we were both too hungry to say anything. We scarfed down our plates then loaded them into the dishwasher.

I dropped my jacket over the back of the couch and loosened my tie before I sat on the couch. I usually showered after I got home from work, but tonight I was too drained to care about completing my regular activities.

Rome sat beside me and kicked off her heels. She always massaged her feet because her shoes killed her feet, but yet, she continued to wear them. The stupidity drove me crazy sometimes. The only reason why I didn't say anything was because she looked damn fine in those five-inch stilettos.

"Jackson is kind of a sweetheart," she said quietly.

"Yeah. He tries to act macho, but he's really a pussy."

She sent me a glare because she didn't care for my cold comment. "Calloway."

When she gave me that no-bullshit attitude, I couldn't help but respect her. No one else ever stood up to me, not even Jackson. "He has a big heart. He tries to hide it all the time, but it's definitely there."

"You're both very sweet."

That was debatable. Jackson and I both got off on whipping women, so we weren't exactly Prince Charming.

"I think a real man wears his heart on his sleeve. I think a real man should love his mother. And I think a real man shows his feelings without caring what anyone thinks. Both of you are that way."

"For the most part." But we both possessed darker sides. If I could kill Hank and get away with it, I would. If I could have killed my dad before he'd had the chance to hurt my mother and me, I would have. Just because I hadn't committed any sins didn't mean I wouldn't have, given the opportunity. I treated Rome with respect only because she demanded it. If she were a different woman, I would expect a perfect submissive or walk away. "With a few exceptions."

"Well, I think you're the greatest man I've ever known." She held my gaze as she said it, showing her sincerity. The affection was in her eyes, the look she gave me countless times during the day. It was the same expression she gave me when we made love. I knew exactly what it meant—that she loved me.

I loved seeing that look.

"I think you're the greatest woman I've ever known." I leaned toward her and pressed my lips against her neck. The second my mouth was on her skin, my body flushed with heat. It burned my lips and made my mouth ache for more.

Rome's body reacted to mine, and her hands touched me everywhere, moving up my arms until she reached the buttons of my shirt. She undid each one, popping them open until the shirt came loose. "Make love to me…" Her lips moved against my ear, her voice deep and seductive.

She never needed to ask me to do such a thing, but I loved hearing the demand anyway. I wanted my woman to want me as much as I wanted her. I wanted to give exactly what she wanted to take.

I moved her to the cushions of the couch and got her ready underneath me, not even bothering to take off all my clothes before I got inside her. My slacks and boxers were pulled over my ass, and my shoes were still on. Her panties were pulled to the side because there wasn't time to remove them.

I shoved myself inside her, and that's when the

connection began. That exquisite alignment of heartbeats, the deep breathing we both shared, and the excitement that neither one of us could contain ran wild through both of us.

Now she was all I could think about.

And I was all she could think about.

## 15

## CALLOWAY

Jackson called me at work later that week. I assumed he wanted to tell me he would visit Mom more often, but that wasn't how the conversation went.

"Do you think you could swing by and help me with a few things?"

I didn't want to take Rome back in there again. When we'd dragged Jackson out of there, it was still awkward. There was no way we could both set foot inside that place and not think about what happened in the playroom. "Can't we take care of this now—over the phone?"

"So, I'm supposed to read off everything to you?" he asked incredulously. "No, I've got more important shit to do."

I rolled my eyes because I knew we were back to

where we were. He was going to act like the conversation we had about Mom never happened. "How long is this gonna take? Can I leave Rome in the car?"

"Just take her home. You're telling me she can't be alone for thirty minutes?"

I didn't like it when she was alone for even one minute.

"Hank obviously isn't a problem anymore. You scared that bitch-face off for good. So drop her off and stop by, alright?"

"Fine."

Jackson hung up without saying goodbye.

Wish I could say I was surprised—but I wasn't.

I was only going down there because I was attached to Ruin. Even if I wasn't running it anymore, I still cared about it. I wanted it to be in good hands. That place had been home to me for so long. I met a lot of friends there, a lot of submissives. It definitely had a place in my heart, as strange as that sounded. If Jackson needed help with a completely different business, I would have hung up a long time ago.

I finished the workday then picked up Rome at her office. We made it to the elevator without touching, but once those doors were shut, I cupped her face and kissed her on the lips. There was a camera in the corner, but that didn't stop me from doing whatever I wanted.

I pressed her against the back wall as I kissed her, our bodies slowly descending to the ground floor of the building. Rome didn't tell me to back off. She kissed me with the same slow passion, her lips giving me purposeful kisses that were innately sexy. I wished I could stop by her office whenever I wanted, just for a kiss, so making out in the elevator would have to suffice.

When we hit the ground floor, the doors opened and we walked to the car.

"I'm going to Ruin for about thirty minutes," I announced once we were in the back seat. "Tom will drop you off at the house then come pick me up." We were already on the way to Ruin, moving in the opposite direction of my home.

Rome didn't seem concerned about it. "Okay. I'll get dinner started."

Even though she didn't ask any questions, I elaborated. "Jackson said he wanted me to help him out with a few things."

"You're the best person to ask. You ran that place for years."

I wasn't sure if I expected her to disagree with my

decision, but I was surprised by her reaction all the same. "You'll be okay at the house by yourself?"

She had the nerve to roll her eyes. "Calloway, I'm not scared in the least. I'll be perfectly fine."

Rome's fearlessness was what attracted me to her in the first place. When Hank assaulted her, she fought back and got away—multiple times. She didn't roll over and play dead. She had a fire that couldn't be put out with a fire hose. "Okay."

Tom pulled up to the club and waited for me to get out. I turned to her. "I'll see you soon, sweetheart."

"Alright." She leaned over the seat and kissed me on the mouth.

The second I felt her lips, I wanted to go home. "Don't tease me, alright?"

"If I wanted to tease you, I'd do this…" She yanked down the front of her dress, showing her perky tits.

My face hardened with frustration and arousal.

"Don't worry." She leaned back and crossed her legs. "They'll be ready for you when you get back."

"Better be." I got out and shut the door behind me. The bouncer immediately stepped to the side and allowed me entry with just a nod for a greeting. I buttoned the front of my suit as I walked into the darkness. Even though it was still early in the evening, there were already people dancing under the black light. Music thudded from the speakers and immersed me in the world I'd been born into.

I walked to the office and hoped I wouldn't run into Isabella on the way. I hadn't seen her since she dropped by my office about a month ago. I was ashamed to admit she tempted me, not because I missed her or wanted her, but because I wanted that relationship with Rome.

I rapped my knuckles against the door before I walked inside. "Where do we start?"

Jackson left the desk and walked back into the hallway. "Follow me."

We crossed the bridge that overlooked the first floor and headed to the other side of Ruin where the playrooms were stationed. Jackson fished out his key card then walked to one of the playrooms reserved for either of us or VIPs.

"What's this about?" I asked, trying not to jump to the wrong conclusion.

"You'll see." He got the door open and stepped into the dark room.

I followed behind him and waited for the lights to be flicked on.

Jackson hit the switch then pressed his body against the door, as if he was blocking it.

I didn't like that one bit. "What are you doing?"

He crossed his arms over his chest then nodded to the center of the room.

Isabella sat on her knees, wearing a leather top and leather shorts with black heels on her feet. Her hair was in a braid over one shoulder, just the way I liked. As if we were back in time, she was ready for me.

I turned back to Jackson and practically snarled. "What the fuck, Jackson?"

"Just listen to me before you flip." He raised one hand like that might steady me. "You let the Dom go free sometimes. If you bottle him up for too long, bad shit will happen. Trust me on that."

"Move away from the door, or I'll make you."

Jackson held his ground even though he knew I could kick his ass. "There's no harm in it. Be who you are then go home to Rome."

"What the fuck?" I snapped. "I thought you liked Rome?"

"I do like her—a lot," he countered. "Which is why you need to do this. If you don't balance out your needs, it'll never work between you two. You can be a good boyfriend to her most of the time—but not all the time. You've done everything you can to make Rome budge, but she won't compromise. If she doesn't want anything to do with the lifestyle, then fine. But she better expect you to get it elsewhere."

I wasn't sure what caused me to hold my tongue. I stared my brother down before I looked at Isabella, who was on her knees with her gaze averted like the perfect submissive she was.

My hands formed fists.

My knuckles turned white.

My breathing became sporadic.

Like a child tempted with candy, I struggled to resist.

"There's no sex." Jackson left the door when he realized the cogs in my mind were turning. "There's no touching. But you get to be who you're supposed to be. I'm doing this because I'm your brother. Rome is great, she really is. But you need more than that. If you aren't going to give her up, then at least this will make you happy—for the long term."

I wanted to say no and walk away. There wasn't an obstacle in the doorway, so all I had to do was storm out. Even if Jackson was in the way, I could just knock him to the side. The only reason why I was still in that room was because I wanted to be.

And I knew that.

Jackson watched me carefully, knowing the devil deep inside me was rearing its horns and coming to life. "You aren't doing anything wrong. You can just tell Rome you're coming to Ruin to help me with a few things once in a while. It's not totally a lie…in a way." He came to my side then looked at Isabella. "You know she's the perfect submissive. She wants to be punished. She wants you to rule her. You want it… she wants it. Just do what feels right, you know?" Like the devil, Jackson sat on my shoulder and whispered terrible things into my ear. He tried to manipulate me with his persuasiveness, understanding me better than almost anyone else. "It's not cheating, Calloway."

But it wasn't right either.

My hands couldn't stop shaking.

I wasn't aroused, but I was still on fire. I felt the heat spread throughout my entire body, the unfulfilled need sweeping over me in a wave. Rome was my whole world, but I would be lying if I said I didn't need more.

I did need more.

Jackson waited for me to do something, to make a decision. When he grew tired of waiting, he went to the stand of whips and floggers and searched through the inventory until he grabbed a dull gray whip sitting on the far right. He grabbed it and examined the texture of the leather in his hand, feeling the material in his fingertips. He smacked the whip gently against his hand as he tested it.

His eyes locked to mine before he walked back

toward me, the whip clutched in his hand. He stopped in front of me then extended it, offering it to me.

I eyed the whip without taking it, feeling my hands shake with adrenaline. Seeing that whip tested my resolve. I wanted to whip Isabella so hard, to make up for the months that I'd been doing nothing but vanilla. My breathing grew more erratic, and I slowly felt my mind slip away, the carnal monster inside me taking control of the man underneath.

Jackson grabbed my hand and forced the whip into my fingertips.

When I felt the leather, I knew I was a goner.

I automatically squeezed it, making my knuckles turn white around it. My breath came out shaky, my chest aching when the air left my lungs. The sweat that formed on my face and my neck suddenly felt overwhelming. I wanted control, craved it with my entire being. I wanted to punish Isabella for all the things Rome wouldn't allow me to do to her. I disintegrated into a new world, a void that was only black and full of nightmares. My compassion and humility slipped away, an arrogant bastard remaining behind.

I tested the whip in my hand then circled Isabella, coming behind her and staring at the bare skin of her back. Fury suddenly overtook me, remembering all the rage I worked so hard to repress. Violence was my craving, and I didn't want to stop until I got it. Rome was no longer on my mind as the beast came forward. "Up." I spoke with more authority than I'd had in the last nine months. It felt right. It felt real.

Isabella rose to a stand, her eyes still on the floor.

Jackson leaned against the wall and smiled.

I pulled my arm back then unleashed a powerful force, smacking her hard right along the back. I hit the skin and turned it blood-red, doing enough damage to the skin that it would last until morning.

And I slipped away.

Isabella cried out then moaned an instant later, feeling the pain and enjoying it at the same time.

I finally felt like myself. I finally felt like Calloway Owens—the Dom.

I truly felt alive.

So I whipped her again.